A Witch's Fury

Kim Bair

Facebook: facebook.com/kimbairauthor
Instagram: KimBairAuthor
Email: kimbair@proton.me
Website: www.kimbair.com
Telegram: KimBairAuthor
Copyright © Kim Bair 2015
Ebook Cover Design by http://www.ebooklaunch.com

More reading goodness by Kim Bair:
    Dead Shifter Walking, The Succubus Executioner Book 1
    Demigod Down, The Succubus Executioner Book 2
    A Witch's Fury, The Succubus Executioner Book 3
    A Council of Betrayal, The Succubus Executioner Book 4
    Death of a Succubus, The Succubus Executioner Book 5
    Legacy of the Succubus, The Succubus Executioner Book 6
    Creation of the Dual Shifter, The Dual Shifter Executioner
    The Mel Files
    Andy's Origin, The Andromalius Chronicles

Table of Contents

Chapter 1

Blake held me lovingly in his arms as we stood on his driveway, about to leave for Kass and Darren's wedding. I hungrily clenched fistfuls of his white dress shirt as he pressed his soft lips firmly against my own, seducing my mouth, one tongue stroke at a time.

I could think of a better place for those strokes.

Groaning, I pressed myself against his well-built form, enjoying his hands kneading the flesh under my t-shirt. His lips curled into a smile that I could feel against my ravished mouth. Untangling my hold, he threaded his fingers through my own before bringing my hands to my sides. Biting on my bottom lip, I scooted forward, pressing my breasts against the fabric I was just trying to wrinkle.

Releasing my hands, he stroked my face with those talented fingers—which I could also find a better place for. Gazing into his blue eyes, dazzling in the afternoon light, I whispered huskily, "I think we should go back inside." A magnetic force drew my eyes back to his perfect lips.

His smile grew as his roaming hands moved to comb back my newly dyed dark brown locks with midnight purple highlights. "I like this look on you."

"I can tell." I pulled him in for another kiss.

"Oh, no you don't," he scolded. He gently shoved me toward the passenger door with a sharp slap on the ass. "We can *not* be late for the wedding."

Relenting, I sighed and slid into the heated leather seat.

Today was the day when I had to hold my tongue, not kill anyone, and try, at least, not to insult anyone.

I scowled. "Being on my best behavior is so not fun."

Weeks after wrapping up the insanity of the sadistic demigod Nari and helping Kass get acquainted with the packs and their lifestyle, we had finally arrived at the wedding day. I was excited to be her maid of honor, proud to stand beside her on this most sacred occasion, even if I had to play nice.

My heart still broke for her that the rest of her wedding party had abandoned her when a few select shifters took issue with a shifter marrying a succubus. We certainly were not the mainstream Supernaturals who announced their existence to the public, but I had created a small dominion by controlling the Supernatural Council. Apparently, a few still thought of us as "demon whores." The truth was that our power lay in our ability to influence emotions; although we couldn't force a feeling into a being, we could easily manipulate and coerce.

I'd like to think I've always used my powers for good, but I'm not that delusional.

...

"Does the caterer have the hors d'oeuvres out in the cantina area?" Kass hollered from the large bathroom of her bridal suite, as she changed into her undergarments.

"Yes, I checked myself," I yelled back, slipping into my own dress in the empty main room.

"Hannah is in her dress?"

"Yep, she is out there with Grandma Jane and Grandpa Lee being doted on." I slid the side zipper up carefully, smoothing out the soft fabric against the curves of my body.

"Does Jane have her corsage?"

My hands abruptly stopped as I considered the question. "I think so."

"Logan and Darren have their boutonnieres?" The bathroom door opened a crack.

"Yes, I pinned them on myself."

"Zip me up?" She asked kicking out the hem of her dress as she held the top up.

"Absolutely, beautiful." I grinned at her foolishly, excited for such a girlie event.

"I hope it still fits," Kass worried, smoothing the dress around her growing baby bump.

"There," I finished. "It fits perfectly." Kass exhaled a relieved sound before turning her critical eye to her hair and makeup.

Standing behind her, I rested my chin on her shoulder, meeting her gaze of equal parts worry and excitement in the mirror. "You look amazing, Kass." As happy as I was for her, I was also secretly jealous.

Kass continued her critical perusal before looking back at me and drawing a deep breath.

"Thank you, Olivia." She blinked back the moisture in her eyes as I squeezed her arm. We left volumes unsaid between us, but our bond as succubi, even with our shields pressed solidly into place, allowed us to feel just a pinch of each other's emotions.

That was enough for us.

Some people will claim that connection makes our kind demons. Since I've never put any stock in religious jargon and have yet to suck anyone's soul, I'm going to call that particular myth false.

The door to the bridal room slammed open. Lorraine, Logan's fiancée who absolutely adored calling me a demon, sauntered in reeking of alcohol. She was dangerously close to spilling her drink down the front of her dress and everything else in the vicinity.

I didn't need this.

I marched over and closed the door behind her with enough force to rattle the pane of glass.

"What could you possibly fucking want?" I growled, crossing my arms over my chest.

Lorraine crashed herself in one of the L shaped couches, spilling her drink on her black dress. The fabric fit snugly against her perfectly shaped body. I felt Kass's self-confidence dip slightly and scowled at Lorraine as I repeated my question, punctuating each word with venom, "What. Do. You. *Want*?!"

She shrugged, unconcerned that the Executioner was currently thinking of various ways to hide her body. Running a hand through her long, straight, raven locks, she confessed, "The boys kicked me out."

"I wonder why," I muttered sarcastically. I turned back to Kass, forcing a smile and locking down my emotions, hoping I did so deeply enough that she wouldn't feel them.

"I feel sick," Kass complained, holding her stomach.

"Ginger ale?" I asked.

She nodded and sank down gracefully on the long, flowered sofa under the picture window.

With a glare at Lorraine, I grabbed my bag and stomped off to the bar in my ballerina flats. I would have preferred my steel-toed boots, but I had to agree with Kass and Jerry that they did clash.

A few guests had already made an appearance, lingering around the exquisite fountain and rustic benches. The entire venue was beautiful: lush trees, flowering bushes, and delicate lighting gave this city locale the feel of a secluded secret garden.

Making my way to the cantina, I smiled at the waitress. "We haven't opened yet," she informed me as she quickly stocked beer.

"I know. I was hoping I could get a ginger ale for the bride. Her stomach is upset," I said, plastering on a bubbly smile.

"Oh, yeah, I think I have some in the back," she said, pulling out a can. "It's a little warm still."

"It's perfect, thank you," I told her sincerely.

Before heading back to Kass, I detoured to the Groom's room, knocking gently on the door before pulling it open.

"Everyone decent?" I called out.

Logan moved into my line of view, his caramel locks cut and styled. "Everything okay?" he asked, pulling on the cuff of his black suit. Oh goodness, did he look suave. It took me a moment to answer as my eyes roved over his powerful thighs, shown off by the tailored black pants, along with those damn alluring raw sienna eyes.

His eyes met mine briefly before they skirted over my dress, taking a long few moments to drag back to my own eyes, sea green.

"Yeah," I said, shaking my head clear. I recovered quickly, pulling out a long, slender, plum package from my bag, walking toward him with the gift extended.

"What is it?" Logan asked warily, turning the package over in his hands.

"A gift," I informed him. Feeling a bit insecure, I crossed my arms over my beautiful dress and retreated to stand in the doorway. I had lost my nerve when I was here earlier, pinning the boutonnieres on.

He arched an eyebrow as he pulled open the package. Holding up the dagger and sheath, he gave me a quizzical look.

"I don't need weapons, I grow talons and fangs. Remember?" he asked. "Did the tango with the demigod damage your memory, or have you perhaps gotten soft hanging around town for the past few weeks?"

I huffed, "It's not for you, dense shifter. It's in case we run into trouble here and I need it. I can't hide it in this dress," I informed him, uncrossing my arms

4

and gesturing at myself so he could see the sheer fabric. "Not to mention that throwing knives will only do so much." I slid the slit of my dress over, revealing my upper thigh encased by the delicate leather strap holding my four throwing knives.

"Oh." Logan said softly, his eyes running over my body. Before my imagination could dwell on the heat in that look, I turned.

"Well I gotta go, be sure that Lorraine doesn't harass Kass in my absence." I fled the room, letting the door slam shut behind me.

I crossed the short distance between the two rooms and handed Kass the ginger ale. She sipped the lukewarm drink while I sat on the arm of the couch, stroking her back.

After a few more sips, she rallied. "Okay, let's get my veil on so we can get the pre-wedding pictures taken."

I nodded. Crossing the room and pulling open the pristine white box resting on the round table, I gently pulled out the intricate lace veil.

Turning with care, I was watchful that I didn't drag the beautiful material on the floor. I stopped truly dumbfounded when Lorraine hauled herself up off of the couch, her wine glass sloshing wildly again. Shaking my head in annoyance, I cemented my forced smile into place before meeting Kass's gaze as she stood in front of the floor length mirror.

Carefully, I tucked the comb into her beautiful dark curls, fluffing the veil around her shoulders and midway down her back

"Perfect." I stepped back, smiling as I pulled the veil over her shoulders.

"Can you grab me the small mirror?" Kass asked, pointing at the round table. I made my way to the table, curling my lip in disgust. Lorraine had found a new place to spill her wine: the flowered couch arm, which she leaned on unsteadily, her eyes half closed.

A knock sounded and the photographer peeked her perky head in. "All ready when you ladies are!"

I nodded, turning to bring Kass the mirror.

Lorraine launched herself off the couch and cut off my path, stumbling as she reached over and adjusted Kass's veil. I swallowed my growl of annoyance.

"Lorraine, can you sit down?" Kass batted at her hands and edged away. "I don't want wine on my dress."

Ha! Take that, Lorraine!

Lorraine yanked back her hand and slapped Kass across the face with her obnoxiously large engagement ring. Blood pooled from the corner of Kass's split lip. The realization that Lorraine had scored first blood came slowly. I was stilled by sheer, stupid shock.

"No," I gasped, horrified.

The blood of our kind holds immense power. When vampires feed off of us it is an intoxicating, nutritious high for them. However, the results of drawing our blood can also be disastrous. In a moment of passion, it enhances the throes of desire; in hatred and anger, nothing good can come of it.

Selena, the psychotic vampire bitch who had created, enslaved, and trained me, had drawn my blood repeatedly until I could control the effects, could focus through the immediate intense emotions and so hone my abilities. It was one of the very few things she had done in my fucked up beginnings that I was grateful for.

Kass never had such training.

"No," I whispered again as the small mirror slid through my boneless fingers to land at my feet. "No!" I screamed louder, getting the attention of Darren and Logan, who burst through the door.

Ignoring their panicked expressions, I flung myself in front of Kass, facing her with arms braced wide.

Kass turned slowly from the mirror, her eyes burning with hatred. She ignored me, her gaze locked onto Lorraine with a need to kill vibrating off her body in powerful waves. Her ruby red painted lips pulled back from her white teeth in a snarl. Her body crouched slightly into the fighting stance I had taught her.

"What happened?!" Logan and Darren yelled together.

"Lorraine drew first blood," I whispered as Kass attempted to launch around me.

Holding her back easily, I settled into my own stance.

"How do we fix this?" Darren asked, standing next to me, his voice colored with worry for his soon-to-be wife.

"Usually I drain both parties within an inch of their lives," I responded, letting him take Kass's next advance. He held her wiggling body against his own until she flung herself backwards.

He turned to me, ashen.

"I am not doing that because of the baby," I assured him. He turned back to Kass.

"I could let Kass kill her," I muttered.

"That bitch hits me!" Lorraine yelled, pointing an accusing finger at me. "Why can't I hit the slut?"

Yeah, I've hit Lorraine a lot. Trust me, she deserves it.

I cringed as Kass renewed her efforts and slammed into my body.

"Get Lorraine out of here!" I bellowed to Logan, foolishly expecting him to listen.

Turning to Darren I said, "I am going to drain her emotionally, that won't hurt the child and should place her in an unnatural calm."

"I'm okay with killing her," Darren answered, his own eyes glowing with hatred at Lorraine.

"Me too," I answered, looking at Kass with a sigh. "But she won't be."

"If I kill her?" Darren asked hopefully as he turned to look at Lorraine, whom Logan still hadn't removed.

I shook my head, "Won't help, but thanks for offering." Kass came at me again, spewing obscenities at Lorraine while trying to claw her way around me.

Wrapping my arms around her slim shoulders, I ducked my head into her neck, sucking a breath and holding it. My power reached out and I quickly pulled Kass's anger, disgust, and hatred to me, letting them mingle with my own emotions, then cramming it all into a metal ball inside of my head.

I was scared to pull back and see whether what I had done worked. The pull was dangerously fast. It would have been easy for me to pull too much or not enough. I was betting on my experience to see us both out of this crisis unscathed. If she hated me for what I had done, I'd understand. Perfectly.

"I'm sorry Kass," I whispered, releasing the breath I was holding. Pulling back, I braced for the results of my handiwork. I had just deprived Kass of all her emotions from this day and several more to come. Kass's eyes found mine and instead of the intelligent, witty, sparkling joy I had seen there just moments earlier, only emptiness remained: a forced calm, forced by my hand.

I pulled my arms off of her shoulders, wrapping them around my middle instead, bowing my head as I took a few steps back. Her emotions roiled inside of me, wanting an outlet, wanting Lorraine's blood to be spilled until the lifeless look in her eyes would soothe my soul.

Clenching my jaw, I closed my eyes, sucking in a deep breath and commanding those desires to lay still. I dug my fingernails into the soft flesh of my palms, willing myself not to draw my throwing knives.

Fucking weddings.

"What about Lorraine?" Darren asked, helping Kass to sit. I hated myself for the blank expression on Kass's face.

It took me a few moments to focus on his question rather than the guilt in my gut.

"She'll need to be drained," I answered. I searched for my phone to text Blake. I was glad to have a menial task to take my mind off what I had just done. I did not want to deal with this shit today of all days. What was wrong with Lorraine? Why didn't I just kill her? The searing heat of first blood warmed my body at the thought of breaking her slender neck with my hands.

Blowing out a breath, I was startled by the door bursting open again. I looked up to see Blake standing there, handsome and regal, his eyes glowing amber.

"This is going to hurt," he hissed, before using his vamp speed to secure his fangs into Lorraine's neck. I smiled at her whimper of pain.

Have I mentioned how much I love that man?

Logan moved to interfere, but Darren's growl stilled the Alpha. Unsure of what to do, Logan opted to stand there, unwanted, glaring at Blake. He may be the Alpha over shifters in the entire U.S., but what Lorraine had done merited punishment.

A wave of jealously washed over me, blinding me with the need to kill Lorraine. Leaning heavily against the couch, I blew out a breath and secured those emotions down deep.

Blake released Lorraine roughly, his face contorted in disgust. She fell, limply, onto the couch behind her.

"You should probably call someone to take care of her," Blake stated indifferently, holding out a hand to me.

"You alright?" he asked, pulling me close. Linked to me from our bedroom activities, he felt an echo of my emotions.

I nodded, forcing a smile, not looking at Kass. I already hated myself for what I had done to her. The chances of her hating me when this was over were high as well.

The chipper photographer popped her head back in. "We ready?"

All eyes turned to Kass, who smoothed down her hair before standing. "Yes, we are," she replied, far too calm.

Chapter 2

We successfully completed all the required pictures. The groom was waiting with the minister or preacher or whatever. I smiled down at Hannah, Darren's daughter. The death of her mother, Darren's first wife, had awakened Hannah's dormant succubus powers. Now she was going to be Kass's adopted daughter. I was thrilled Hannah would have such a teacher and guardian.

"You ready?" I asked in an excited whisper as music began playing.

She nodded, crossing her arms in her delicate light purple dress and smooshing the basket of flower petals against her. "I was born ready," her saucy butt informed me.

I smothered a laugh as I said, "You have been spending too much time with me."

She shrugged. Holding her head high, tossing petals regally, she gracefully walked the aisle to her father. I love that kid.

As I turned to Kass, my smile fell away. She looked at me blankly. "I should smile?" she questioned.

"Only if you want to."

My own smile felt rigid and, like Kass's, didn't reach my eyes.

...

The ceremony was elegant, just like Kass. Darren gazed adoringly at Kass during the exchange of vows and I, thankfully, couldn't see Kass's face as she gave hers. Her bland voice had me cringing internally, though.

We finally sat down to eat. I could now relax the smile that was straining my cheek muscles. I let out a breath and commenced inhaling the food that was laid out before us, not tasting much as my mind replayed the scene with Lorraine. It really might be time to kill the bitch. However, killing humans is frowned upon, not to mention that I'd have to deal with the fallout with Logan.

Casting a look at Logan, who sat on the other side of Darren at the long table, I drummed my fingers against the cream tablecloth, deep in thought.

I watched the waiter lean forward to whisper something into Logan's ear. Based on the stiffening in his shoulders and the twitch in his jaw, it wasn't good news. He pushed his chair back forcefully and followed the skinny human help to the kitchens.

I waited a moment, watching them, before I decided to follow. Let's be honest, I don't really trust Logan to be able to handle much of anything, and when it came to Kass's big day, I wouldn't be letting the overgrown shifter screw it up.

Not that I hadn't already screwed it up, but that was beside the point now. Pushing through the swinging double doors and advancing down the long hallway, I found the kitchen. Logan's voice bouncing off the small space had me turning right down another corridor, where I caught up to him.

"What's going on?" I asked, coming up next to him and scanning the shifters lined up in front of him. "Really Logan," I complained, "can't I leave you alone for two minutes?"

"Apparently, these folks have a problem with a succubus marrying into the family," he informed me, never taking his eyes off the angry shifters facing us.

"Bring it on boys," I challenged. Fangs began to sprout from the angry group of idiotic shifters. Their eyes emitted an intense glow that illuminated the dimly lit hallway.

Moving a hand to Logan's back I pulled out my blade, as his hands simultaneously sprouted talons. I huffed, jealous of both his fangs and razor sharp claws.

The first two moved with impressive speed as they lunged, snarling at us. I braced my legs wide for the impact. Logan, however, leapt in front of me, taking the brunt of the hit. His powerful shoulders bunched under the effort to keep from being shoved back.

Not one to miss a fight, I kicked out at the closest one, thankful for the floor-to-hip slit in my dress, landing a solid hit to the solar plexus. The shifter's air whooshed out of his body, bending him forward. Following my kick with an upper cut, I sent the first idiot onto his back with a bloody nose.

"I can't believe I have to save your ass yet again!" I yelled at Logan in the tiny hallway, as I slammed the second idiot's head into the plaster.

Okay, so I was enjoying myself, a little bit.

"I didn't ask for your help," he barked at me, breaking the arm of his attacker.

"No, you just brought the fight to a location where you knew I would be," I answered, slamming my foot between the thug's legs, grinning evilly when his eyes bugged out of his head.

Spinning, I wheeled my elbow into the original idiot's temple, dropping him for a second and final time.

"I am perfectly capable of handling this myself," Logan growled, body slamming his next attacker with ease.

I shrugged, realizing we had dispatched the crowd quickly. "I needed a good fight, anyways," I said, slipping my blade under his jacket for safe storage again.

I hadn't used the blade to do anything more than inflict surface wounds on the idiots. We hadn't killed them, but we had delivered impressive damage; hopefully, the message would be taken seriously by any who disagreed with Kass and Darren's marriage. Besides, killing people at Kass and Darren's wedding seemed pretty terrible, even for me.

"Let's get back," Logan said, turning.

"Whoa, turbo," I advised, pulling him back around.

He looked down at my hand on his bicep, annoyed as I brushed plaster off his shoulder and out of his hair.

"Am I wearing any plaster?" I asked, hands on my hips.

"No," he responded curtly, turning back to storm down the hallway.

...

If I thought I had been excited to sit down and eat, then I was ecstatic when we ushered Kass and Darren through a tunnel of sparklers to their awaiting limo.

My final duties were to clean up, and to gather and deliver gifts. Once I completed those tasks, I headed outside to find Blake.

He was leaning against a pillar looking around at the peaceful landscaping. Slipping up behind him, I wrapped my arms around his waist, a contented sigh passing over my lips.

"Penny for your thoughts?" I asked softly.

Resting his hands over my own he said, "Do you ever want to be married?" He didn't look back at me.

I rested my cheek against his shoulder, thinking about the question before I answered. "I never thought I would find anyone I wanted to marry, until I met you." I hesitated, realizing I had just opened up a piece of my heart to him.

Blake turned in my arms, smiling softly as he leaned down to kiss me gently, stroking my cheek. He leaned back, searching my eyes before turning us to head toward the car. I hadn't asked him the same question. I was afraid of the answer. I was afraid this wedding had made him realize that I wasn't marriage material, and I was not ready for the beautiful bubble to come crashing down around me.

Chapter 3

It had been a long time since I had pissed off Grams this badly.

Granted, since I had pulled her from destitution as a cocaine addicted, poor excuse of a madam of a drug-infected whorehouse, she typically put up with all my shit rather well.

"I cannot believe you used George to catch Governor Hash with prostitutes," she stated yet again, eyes clenched closed, fingers massaging her temples.

Tilting my head, I watched her strained expression. "Don't forget the drugs," I added. I was impressed with my creativity in using my human pimp contact to trap Governor Hash in drug and prostitution charges. Hey, I didn't kill the asshole. That is progress.

She groaned, still not looking at me.

"What's the big deal? The man deserved far more than the slap on the wrist he is receiving now. He propositioned me in the alleyway of Kitten," I reminded her, still mortified, annoyed, and wanting to kill the man.

Grams finally lowered her hand from her face, regarding me with cold, slate eyes. I stared back. I was missing something.

"What?" I asked again, leaning forward in the uncomfortable blue chair.

Grams blew out a breath. "Nothing. Just the devil we know is better than the devil we don't."

"He kept his job," I reminded her, cracking my neck. I muttered, "Amazingly enough," under my breath.

Grams shrugged, meeting my gaze, "He is powerful, Olivia. You would do well to remember that." With that, she turned back to her computer.

My eyes narrowed. Did Grams just threaten me? That certainly didn't sound like just a warning. Before I could voice my suspicions, she threw a file at me.

"I'm aware you wanted to take a break, but I need you on this one." Her slate gray eyes regarded me levelly, giving us both a graceful way out.

I snatched it from her desk before storming out.

I've never been graceful.

...

I looked over the file from Grams again while sitting in my SUV outside the manor, annoyed with myself for not checking where I was going. The miserable state of Ohio and I do not get along. I skimmed the pages again, looking for what type of supernatural I was going up against, again not finding an answer. Strange, considering that the rest of the file was robust in minute details about the child I was to obtain, Mindy, from her abusive and elusive stepfather.

With a groan I cranked the engine, punching the address into my GPS. The sooner I was done the better.

...

The drive had taken me seven long hours. Looking up at the dilapidated row of houses in front of me, I debated calling Grams at this ungodly hour, but decided against it. I certainly didn't want to interrupt her time with Mercer. I'd call tomorrow during normal business hours.

Leaning back in my seat, I tapped the steering wheel, debating. Should I check into a hotel or sit here and hope the offending Supernaturals showed their faces before I needed to sleep?

Assuming I could easily identify them, I could handle this child abuse case and get the hell out of here.

Leaning my head back against the headrest, I adjusted my rearview mirror so it gave me a clear view of the house. Decision made.

...

I didn't have to wait long. Thank all the Gods, I lack the patience.

Two figures huddled against the fresh falling snow, one a child, the other a larger figure who opened the half-fence and shoved the child in. The child stumbled and fell. I growled low in my throat, watching the adult laugh. I had been spending too much time around the damn shifters.

I couldn't see the child's face, but I watched her intently as the standing figure pulled back a leg, slamming it into her frail form. It took all my limited self-control not to tear that leg from his body right there on the street. Not that in this neighborhood anyone would lift a finger to help, or that such acts of extreme violence would even elicit a response, but I refrained.

The steering wheel creaked beneath my hands and I forced a breath out of my lungs, waiting as the lights in the house came on and went off.

Releasing my cramped hands from the steering wheel, I flexed the stiff digits before easing out of the SUV and closing the door gingerly. Waiting a frosty second, I scanned the neighborhood for any witnesses before I crunched through the freshly fallen snow to the back of the house. Nothing stirred inside or out as I used my lock pick set to ease the squeaky-hinged door open, silently cursing it.

The house was a disaster: partially eaten meals dried onto plastic plates, pizza boxes ripped open and the contents strewn about. The kitchen sink was unusable under a mound of filthy dishes. My nose wrinkled in disgust at the smell as I cautiously moved over the threadbare carpet of undetermined color and down the narrow hall.

I should have seen it coming, but I didn't, which was why the blow to the back of my head knocked me into complete darkness.

...

I awoke with a throbbing at the base of my neck as I rolled gingerly from my side to my back on the cold concrete floor. I blinked rapidly to clear my fuzzy vision, until a dark and damp room came into view. With considerably more effort than it should have taken, I raised my head toward the light at the far end of the room, noting the lack of windows. Two figures were hunched over the contents of my SUV, along with my jacket and shoes.

I had heard the rustling of chains, but hadn't realized they were secured around my limbs until I tried to stand, finding I couldn't.

"Dammit, I told you I should have taken a run at her before she woke up," one stated, sealing his death at my hands.

"It doesn't matter, this basement is soundproofed, and she ain't goin' nowhere," the other one reminded him, still sorting through my belongings.

I sat up slowly, resting my arms around my knees that were pulled against my chest, pulling my chains taut. "Where is Mindy?" I asked.

They both turned to my question. "Who's asking?"

"Your personal Executioner."

They jeered at me, stepping closer.

"I love the fighters."

"Not me, I'll stay with the kid."

My hands fisted, "I'm going to enjoy this," I whispered. "Just. Come. Closer." I enunciated each word with deadly intent.

"You'll get your turn," the leader, who liked a fighter, informed me. They were giving me a wide berth as they made their way behind me into the darkness.

"Mindy!" he called out. I shifted to my knees, tracking their progress past me. The manacles around my limbs dug into the skin at my wrists and through the leather on my ankles. I wanted those fuckers dead.

I could hear Mindy shifting behind me in the darkness while I struggled to turn. I could visualize her malnourished, beaten body, the slumped shoulders and the inability to meet her attackers' gaze. I was totally oblivious to the warm blood falling from my wrists as memories of my own horrible childhood competed for my attention.

"No," Mindy's voice was so soft, so plaintive that it broke my fucking heart and renewed my struggle against the chains.

Heat seared from the bonds restraining me yet still I was unaware, wrapping my hand around the chains for additional leverage.

"*Every chain has a breaking point,*" Lord Master informed my fourteen-year-old self, the repressed memories finally winning the fight against my reality.

"Now, do I let the next one in to have a crack at you? Or are you going to actually try this time?" He *paused, laughing in the pristine white room decorated with the ruby red of my blood. "I do know you are enjoying this."*

I was going to kill him. Cold resolve pooled into me, silencing the fear, removing my anxiety that I would die. Until this point I had craved survival, to live, this crazy hope in my chest telling me, screaming at me there was more than the beatings and the rapes, but now I didn't care. I had been pushed too far, had seen too much, had been destroyed beyond measure.

Now, I wanted blood and I wasn't particular regarding to whom it belonged.

Lord Master smiled. It was not a pretty sight as the chains binding me became airborne. I smiled back. This I was going to enjoy.

Mindy's screaming jerked me back to the present and into the inferno raging around us.

"What the hell?" I muttered, casting around into the tall flames for some understanding of what had happened. I coughed, covering my mouth against the thick smoke building from the fiery blaze.

Mindy screamed again and I moved, freely. Apparently, that memory was good for something. In an attempt not to repeat it all again, I looked for a way to Mindy.

I didn't have many options in terms of movement. Whatever had caused the fire had left a clear path for me over the wall of trash, so I took it.

A perfect circle kept Mindy safe, her dark wide eyes reflecting the fire swarming around us.

"Are you okay?" I asked her, physically checking her arms and legs for burns.

"Who are you?" her small voice asked.

"Olivia."

"The Executioner?"

"Only for the bad guys, sweetie. Let's get out of here."

I turned, looking around, my confidence in my ability to perform on my words flagging. Flames snapped at my legs and singed the ends of my hair.

"Can you control it?" I asked hopefully.

"No!" Mindy screamed at me above the roaring sea of flames.

"Shit," I muttered, "hold on tight." This was a terrible plan, and I knew that going in.

Picking up Mindy, I hunched my body around her, hoping like hell I had her vital bits covered before running to the wooden stairs that were quickly being consumed by the greedy inferno.

Terrible plan.

I stormed up the sagging stairs, taking three at a time as I pushed my long legs to the brink of their ability, not stopping when the wood proved too far gone for our weight and plunged in splintering shards to the concrete floor below. Flames kissed my ankle, raw flesh throbbing in unison to my accelerated heart rate, but it couldn't slow me down. I crashed through the closed door, spraying us both with wooden chunks, and hurtled down the hallway toward the putrid kitchen, not pausing at the door to freedom. Holding Mindy tightly, I shifted my shoulder down, demolishing the door from the frame.

With my ankle submerged in the soft snow, dulling the painful throbbing, I finally stopped moving, a blissful sigh escaping my lips.

Setting Mindy down, I took stock of our situation: I didn't have my jacket, didn't have any shoes, no car keys, weapons, or the carefully selected first aid kit. It was all turning to ash in the basement.

"Fuck," I groaned, kicking the snow. Listening to the sirens in the distance, I winced in pain as the skin on my ankle tightened.

"Fuck," I repeated for good measure.

Mindy looked up at me warily. "Let's go kid," I said. "You will be the first fire starter I have brought home."

"I didn't start the fire," she said, taking my offered hand as we made our own path in the freshly fallen snow to my car.

"You certain?"

"Yeah, pretty sure I would have used that trick MONTHS ago."

I didn't have a response for that. I unlatched the half gate for us.

Doors began opening in the neighborhood, the streets filling with spectators as I limped to my Black Beauty—great, now I was naming my vehicles. Thankfully we were largely ignored. Frozen pebbles dug into the soft flesh of my ruined feet. Finally arriving at the SUV, I leaned heavily against the rear driver's side door.

"Any chance you want to get under there and find my spare key?" I gestured to the undercarriage of the SUV.

The look she leveled at me was answer enough.

With a sigh I slid under the carriage. "I know I hid it somewhere," I muttered, hitting pay dirt a few moments later as I pulled the small glorious box out from its magnetized hiding spot on the metal frame.

Wiggling back, I hurried my movements upon seeing the fire department truck flashing up the road and neighbors pointing at us, waving their hands. A few had started toward us. I groaned, tossing the plastic container to the ground and rapidly unlocking the SUV. Mindy didn't need encouragement to hustle into the passenger seat, clambering up the steps. I hauled myself up right after her, then cranked the engine and stomped the accelerator.

I blew out a breath watching the fire disappear from my rearview mirror, the neighbors still pointing at us to the men in the yellow uniforms. I still wouldn't feel comfortable until we had more distance between us. Even if they had my license plate, Grams could handle clean up on this disaster.

"What are you?" I asked Mindy who, not unlike myself, had shoved the bad memories away, putting on a brave face.

"Human." Okay, she was coping with a huge amount of sass.

I blinked several times, pressing my lips into a thin line before a string of creative cursing pried them open. It was time to call Grams. Too bad that wasn't happening, thanks to my lack of a phone.

...

Dusk turned into full dark and I still wasn't stopping. Mindy had long ago fallen into a fitful sleep, small noises coming from her huddled frame against the door. I was still fucking pissed. At Grams for omitting the truth, at myself for losing EVERYTHING, and at the too-quick death of true monsters. It just wasn't a good day.

I wasn't about to think on what Mindy had said, that she was human, and the implications that would have regarding my own magic abilities, abilities I had been doing a great job of ignoring thus far.

I needed supplies, but supplies cost money. I needed to call Grams. I'd prefer to show up, smelling bad and looking worse to really drive home just how pissed I was, but Mindy needed food and a shower.

On the outskirts of Cloverdale, Indiana I was tired enough to pull into a well-lit parking lot of a hotel with a gift shop.

"Stay here," I warned Mindy when her head instantly perked up at the lack of motion.

She apparently had listening issues, along with sass. The sound of her door shutting stopped me mid-stride. I stared daggers into the top of her small head, only partly visible above the SUV. Not wasting my breath on the issue, I walked into the small office.

An older gentleman looked up from his newspaper, smoothing the paper with wrinkled hands, then pausing to push his wire rim glasses back up his nose. "You are some kind of trouble, girl."

"I'll assume you're talking to her," I commented dryly, nodding at Mindy. "I need to borrow a phone."

Rubbing his chin with his first two fingers, he eyed my smoky appearance and damaged, raw flesh, the debate on helping me evident in his gaze. When his eye landed on Mindy, he softened. How often do psychos have small children

20

with them? The answer is more fucking often than I like to think about. People with families can be just as evil as those without.

He pushed the desk phone toward me. I crossed the distance between us, leaning heavily on the counter as I dialed.

"Hello?" a sleepy voice answered.

"Grams," I growled.

"Olie?" I heard the whisper of sheets moving and another muffled voice, Mercer.

"Yes." I wanted to ask, who the fuck else calls at ungodly hours after you send them after a fucking HUMAN? I didn't, mainly because I didn't want to explain to the old man pretending to read his paper.

"Why haven't you called?"

"Why—" I stopped the response, my eyes flicking over to the desk clerk. "I need you to wire me money and pay for a hotel for tonight."

Grams sighed, annoyed. "Can I send money in the morning?"

"Of course, I'm sure Mindy doesn't mind not eating until then."

"You have her?" she asked, breathless and alert.

I held the phone close to my lips, the plastic creaking beneath my fingers. "Of. Course." If only I could convey my irritation and annoyance with those two words alone.

"I'll do it. Hang on."

I pulled the phone away from my ear, staring at it in disbelief.

"Mindy?" Mercer asked, worried.

Finding her close to my hip, I gave her the phone.

"Grandpa?" Her small voice questioned.

"Oh God Mindy," he paused, emotions ceasing his words. Then, "Go with Olivia. Stay with her, she will keep you safe."

Mindy cradled the phone gently, her dark eyes searching mine. "Okay."

It took all my self-control to hand the phone to the clerk and say, "She has the credit card information."

...

Mindy slept with a full belly, freshly cleaned dark locks, and a terrible teal Welcome to Indiana t-shirt with a too-large pair of gray sweats. I had picked up a pocketknife—a terribly made, pathetic item I would personally laugh at in a fight, but it made me feel better as I flicked out the sharpened edge and stowed it again.

My anger had simmered until it wasn't pushing forcefully against my shields, but I was having a hard time understanding why the woman I trusted with my entire organization, my entire life's work, was lying to me. So fucking help her Gods if it was for a man.

···

I intentionally did not pick up the phone Grams had secured for me the next morning, stopping only for the cash, snacks for Mindy, and a first aid kit to wrap my ankle and feet. We were going to talk in person.

I did get myself a sunshine yellow t-shirt and flip flops from the gift store that did not match my leather pants. If only Jerry could see me now. In addition to driving me around on occasion, he was responsible for every adorable item of clothing I owned.

···

Pulling into the manor's cobblestone driveway, I looked up at the front door with a sense of dread eating away at me. I was out and around the SUV while Mindy was still looking up at the building in uncertainty.

"You own a mansion?" she asked, stepping down hesitantly.

"I prefer to call it a manor, and where else would I put the wayward children like yourself?" I tried for a smile, I really did.

She nodded, taking my hand, "So there are kids like me here?"

"Many." Too many.

I gave her hand a squeeze and we walked through the front doors, then straight upstairs to Grams's office.

I debated for half a second on knocking when I heard the voices. Deciding against it, I opened the door wide, pulling Mindy in with me.

"What the ever-loving fuck?" I screamed.

Never in my most paranoid dreams did I ever imagine the man Grams would betray me for would be Hash, sitting relaxed in front of her office. My hands instantly moved to Mindy's shoulders, pulling her close.

"Get out," I hissed, my voice carrying the weight of my anger.

He listened, rushing past me like the slime he was. The death stare I was packing still worked. I turned it to Grams.

"Ex—plain," I demanded, drawing out the syllables.

"It was a meeting," she calmly informed me, pressing down her pale blue suit.

"About what?"

"Business."

"MINDY!" Mercer cried out from behind me. Turning, I watched her own shields crack as she became a hurt little girl again, crumbling into her grandfather's arms.

Grams came around her desk, patting my arm. "Good job."

"I'm not your pet," I hissed at her.

Crossing her arms, she indicated with her eyes the beautiful moment unfolding before us, silently chiding me.

Pulling her deeper into her office, I squeezed her arm with unnecessary force.

"You're hurting me."

I probably should have apologized; Grams had not been scared of me in a long damn time. "What is wrong with you?" I hissed, releasing her.

She covered her fear well, straightening her suit and squaring her shoulders. "I don't owe you anything."

Leaning in close, I clenched my jaw and forced out, "Is that you or Hash talking now?"

Grams shoved me hard enough to back me up.

"What's going on?" Mercer asked, his voice thick with tears.

"This is not over," I snarled before leaving.

If I couldn't stay and yell at Grams for betraying me by having the enemy at a place where I kept our children, and even my warped sense of decency said to give Mercer and Mindy their time together, I was going shopping.

At least that would bring me some measure of pleasure.

...

Myrtle's is not what most would think of when going shopping. The walls are not covered in gun displays, or the lighting fluorescent in color. But this troll, and I do mean that literally, has the most impressive collection of weapons this side of the Mississippi. Not to mention that she energetically cleans them. In this business, that was important and worth her higher-than-normal price tags.

The smoky interior clung to my neon yellow shirt and I groaned as all eyes turned toward me. Let's hope I hadn't used up all the power in my death stare.

"Lord have mercy, Olivia, you look like a woman on a mission." Myrtle's thick voice was sweet music to my ears. Her lavender hair was not complemented by her stone gray skin. Sitting down hid her short stature, but not her thick and strong body.

"Myrtle," I sighed in relief, flopping onto the worn leather couch next to her. Something was going right. My anger had quickly turned to exhaustion.

"Woman, you smell foul."

I lifted a pit to check as several other trolls working took notice. They might have started out in the swamps, but these trolls cleaned up better than I did, obviously.

I shrugged, "It's been an interesting few days. It's also going to be a profitable few hours for you."

Both her purple eyebrows rose. "Special item?"

"All the items," I muttered, leaning my head back and staring at the black ceiling.

"You lost ALL of them?" she asked me, astonished.

"Yeah, I did."

Myrtle sputtered for a few moments. "How?"

"Don't ask," I muttered.

"Alright then, where should we start? Crossbows, swords, throwing knives—I know, follow me."

It took more effort than I am willing to admit to get myself off that couch. My adrenaline and anger were spent. I was empty.

...

Two hours later at the back of my SUV, I admired Myrtle's handiwork.

"Feel better?" She nudged me from her short frame.

"You have no idea." All the glittering gold and diamonds couldn't compare to my joy and feeling of completion seeing the blades, crossbows, and swords stowed in the SUV, shining back at me. I traced my fingers over the sig 1911 pearl grip handles in the black harness fitted over my terrible yellow shirt.

"Thanks, Myrtle."

My equilibrium had been restored.

I supposed I needed actual clothing next.

Clothing and weapons accounted for, I headed to Blake's for a much-needed shower and probably an apology. I had gone radio silent on him as well as Grams. Oops.

Cracking the door open, I slipped in and dropped my large shopping bag by the laundry room before walking quietly into the kitchen.

He was waiting for me, perched at the island with two phones.

I sat next to him at the breakfast counter and watched his nimble hands toy with the phones. My own hands clasped together, shoulders hunched, I felt the weight of my bad decision-making.

"I've been trying to reach you." He didn't look at me.

I spaghetti-slouched deeper into the quicksand the tall chair had become. "Sorry."

He pushed the phone in front of me, along with a replacement credit card from Grams that he pulled from his pocket, before standing. "Hungry?"

"Starved."

He gave me a small, tight-lipped smile, his sapphire blue eyes distracted. "Go get dressed, we have reservations."

I smiled, moving around the counter to press a quick kiss against his cheek. He couldn't be that mad at me if he'd made reservations. But his rigid posture was cause for hesitation. "Everything okay?"

"No," he answered honestly, "but soon it will be."

I didn't push, but my gut was demanding that I launch a shoulder into his walls. I was having a hard time ignoring it.

Chapter 4

The ride to the restaurant was quiet. Blake was unreachable, leaving me with time to think. I replayed my fight with Grams over and over. I didn't like the way things ended between us. Grams is an important constant in my life and, more importantly, in the children's. She has put up with more shit from me than anyone else. I in turn overlooked her expensive wardrobe, dinners out, and vacations. But her lying left me feeling repulsed.

I had a hard time trusting and even greater difficultly forgiving.

Pulling myself back to the present, I smiled at Blake, trying to ease the tension from my shoulders. I had been denied a romp before dinner; however, I had high hopes that only meant he had something delicious and naughty planned for later. I pushed the offensive feelings away, wanting to focus on us. I reached over and stroked the back of his neck casually. Judging by the tension in his own shoulders, things with his family were still not resolved. My smile dipped and my worry blossomed in full force.

When the valet took the car, Blake handed it off without a look or nod of thanks. I tilted my head, watching his unusual behavior as he came around the vehicle.

"Shall we?" he asked, buttoning his suit jacket.

I nodded, noting that he didn't extend an arm for me to take. Actually, he hadn't been touching me very much at all. Was it possible he was still angry about me not having a phone?

The restaurant was beautiful, softly lit and rich with tantalizing scents that teased my taste buds as the hostess sat us at our linen-covered table with delicate crystal centerpieces. I crossed my feet under the table, suppressing a wince as my roughed-up ankle let me know it was none too pleased at being locked into a high heel. It was shocking, but I had broken down and actually worn a pair Blake had picked out. I really didn't want him mad at me. The dress I picked out of my small section of Blake's closet was a favorite little black dress he had surprised me with.

"Good evening," the waiter began, "can I interest you in a drink to begin?"

"We would like the house cabernet," Blake stated, casting a look behind me before returning his gaze to me.

He smiled at me. Warmth pooled into my stomach at the sight, pulling me forward in my chair.

"I hear they make excellent eggplant parmesan," he suggested.

"Think it will pair well with the wine?" I asked, tilting my head at him.

He shrugged. "When have you ever been discriminating about your wine?"

I laughed, "True."

The waiter returned, pouring our drinks as we ordered dinner. I also added dessert.

The meal was delicious. Our conversation flowed and ebbed, the tension draining out of Blake's shoulders. I ate his dinner along with my own, since I would be feeding him later anyway.

He cleared his throat, which is an unneeded act for a vampire. I was about to tease him about getting out of here so he could have his dessert when he looked back over my shoulder, his face falling painfully.

"What's wrong?" I asked, reaching out to lay my hand over his.

"I have something to tell you and it's not pleasant." He wouldn't meet my gaze. Fear stole my breath.

With a determined jaw clench, he raised his head to look at me, and what I saw in his eyes had my heart sinking. I wanted to cry out for him not to say whatever it was, but I sat there mute.

"Olivia, I brought you here to end our relationship." He rushed on, keeping his voice low, "I know I was the one who demanded exclusivity from you." His blue eyes searched my own terrified ones. "I want you to know the things you shared with me in confidence will stay that way."

"What?" I whispered, feeling my chest constrict painfully as I waited for the punch line, blood draining from my face. My entire world narrowed to Blake. This had to be some terrible, awful attempt at a joke, or—or—my mind blanked. I was rendered speechless.

He shook his head, moving his napkin from his lap to the table. "I can't do this anymore, Olivia. I have to make the choices that are best for me and my House, and you are—" he hesitated, searching my face. When he finally met my gaze, uncertainty flickered in his eyes and I could guess why. He was debating how his next words would impact my reduced emotional capacity.

"Damaged," I breathed the word, closing my eyes and bowing my head. Forcing myself to look at him through blurry eyes, I searched my mind for something to say, anything to make him stay. This really was happening. He finally saw me exactly as I am. That thought silenced my unvoiced protests.

"I am so fucking sorry," he whispered, his hands reaching out across the table. My own clutched the fabric in my lap. I felt his hesitation; if he wanted to, he could extend his long arms, breach the distance and touch me, but he didn't. Instead, he pushed back his chair with a screech and fled the restaurant.

It certainly wasn't new information that I was broken. After everything I had confessed, all the terrible memories I had shared with him, I had fooled myself into hoping. It was a foolish hope that another being could love me enough to look past the broken pieces. I knew this moment was coming, had always known that one day the blinders would come off for Blake and he would see me exactly as I am.

Broken.

I was a foolish, hopeful, idiot.

The waiter arrived at the table, awkwardly holding the bill in front of him. "Did he pay?" I asked softly, unable to look at him directly. I wasn't leaking my emotions, but I didn't have to be for him to pick up on my pain. My body language and the tear slipping down my cheek were evidence enough.

"No," he answered softly.

I nodded, pulling out my card, grateful in that moment that Grams had the foresight to leave one along with my phone. The waiter took it quickly, scurrying away. I should have ordered that entire damn bottle, not just the glass I drank. I needed something to numb the pain about now.

The waiter returned swiftly and I forced my brain to focus on the numbers in front of me before I stood to take my leave. What was I paying for anyways, two glasses of wine still in the bottle? It didn't matter, I just wanted to run away and lick my wounds.

What was best for his family? I slammed the pen down on the table. As if I hadn't saved his ass on more than one occasion? What the fuck is wrong with him?

No. What the fuck was wrong with me? Plenty. If I could just be what he wanted, just be what he needed. Biting on my lip, I pushed down my misery. I was damaged, broken beyond repair and Blake deserved better. There was no happy ending in my life.

I needed to accept that.

Heads turned as I left, whispers and snickers following me, but I held my head high. I was falling apart in a pit of self-loathing, but weakness equated to challenges for my title and my life. I could at least keep it together professionally.

I pushed out the glass door and stepped into the chill of the night air.

Something fundamental had changed in me with Blake. Walls I had built around my heart and my past crumbled under his gentle caresses and kind words. For a brief moment, I felt worthy and dammit, even loved.

I was such a fucking fool.

Waiting in line for a cab, I smelled him before I saw him. I closed my eyes and turned my attention downward to my crossed arms. I needed him to leave me the fuck alone. My eyes hadn't quite dried up and I did not need the leader of the Shifter Nation seeing me in this condition.

"Olivia!" Lorraine, his fiancée, called out drunkenly. Fuuuuck.

I pulled my head up to stare at her, unable to utter a word or perform any action in greeting.

"You alright?" Logan asked, stopping short when he saw me.

I shrugged, not trusting my voice or the concern in his caramel eyes. Maybe this whole ugly event could just stay at the restaurant.

"She got dumped, dude," a slurred voice blurted out behind me as Logan handed his ticket to the valet. For the love of the seven hells, please tell me Logan was not in the restaurant witnessing my humiliation.

I closed my eyes to stop the threat of tears and to not kill the drunk behind me.

"Oh, Olie, how terrible!" Lorraine said, coming to put an arm around my shoulders with a drunken sway and a false sense of giving a shit.

Logan pulled her back quickly as my eyes opened to depths of pure insanity, I was certain.

"The fucker didn't even pay the bill," confided the drunk, throwing a companionable arm around my shoulders. "You can do so much better than him, honey," he tried to comfort me.

Keeping Lorraine behind him, Logan eased forward, removing the man's arm tentatively from my shoulder before I had a chance to remove it from his body.

"You probably shouldn't touch her right now," Logan muttered, pulling me to him. I moved stiffly, staring into his eyes, needing a fight.

"Let me give you a ride home," he said cautiously, as though I would snap any moment.

He was right, I might.

I said nothing as the valet drove up in a tiny sports car with a miserably small excuse for a backseat. If not for the drunk still calling out to me, I would have preferred the roomier backseat of a cab, but in my current state I wasn't sure what I was going to do. I knew what I was capable of, however, and that thought made me shove my tall frame into the cramped backseat.

"I hate this car," I murmured under my breath. Actually, I hated a lot. The fancy restaurant, of which I couldn't recall the name, the drunk behind me, but most of all, myself. I couldn't fault Blake for ending it—hell, I could understand. I just had hoped it would last.

Logan sped away from the corner. "Lorraine, move your seat up," he scolded.

She huffed but obliged. "Thanks," I muttered, gaining a precious few inches for my long legs.

"How did you get reservations there, anyways?" she asked hauntingly. Good to know that out of the public eye, she was the same old bitch I detested.

"I didn't," I responded blandly, looking out into the rain-damped night and feeling my heart beginning to shut down. If I was lucky I could rebuild those precious walls, maybe. I would never make the same mistake of letting another in as deeply as I had Blake.

Logan and Lorraine were fighting and I didn't care, couldn't bring myself to give a shit, even when Lorraine lobbed insult after insult at me. She was a lowly, cruel human. I had no use for her.

My phone rang, pulling me from my miserable circle of thoughts. For a split second I hoped it would be Blake, but Grams's name appeared instead.

"Yep," I answered, disappointed.

"Olie, Blake just delivered your things to the manor."

"Yep," I repeated, my heart hollow.

She paused for a moment. "Are you alright?"

"I don't know how to answer that question. I'll be there in a bit." I ended the call, glad our earlier fight had been forgotten, though almost certainly not forgiven.

I had made the decision on a previous case, when a vampire visiting The Centennial House kidnapped Tommy, that I wouldn't be spending any additional time at the manor. Good idea in theory, but over time, I found I was physically and emotionally unable to abide by those rules. The simple fact was that I missed the screaming hellions under my watch, especially Tommy.

Aside from his impressive tech skills, he kept me sane.

So I doubled security instead.

Logan's phone rang and he hit ANSWER on the steering wheel. "What's up, Darren?"

"Did you hear about Olivia?" Worry clouded Darren's voice.

"Yeah, actually we are giving her a ride home," Logan answered while making a turn.

The fast clicking of a keyboard in the background stopped. "I guess I don't need to track her cell phone."

"No, I have her. We will be at the manor in fifteen minutes."

"Did you find her?" Kass's anxious voice broke in over the speakers.

I groaned. "Why is everyone freaking out?" I yelled. "I got dumped, not killed. Fuck. I will be back to the manor any minute."

"Olie, I was worried..." Kass began, her pause telling. Another person carefully wording a response because of my fragile emotional state.

"I'm fine Kass, now really isn't the time," I growled, rubbing my temples. I did not want to be pitied. I might be a broken, rage-fueled, alleged demon, but one man would not shatter me.

"Okay, I'll see you in a bit then," she finished, her relief evident as she ended the call.

"No fucking way," I muttered. I knew the best way to get my mind off the hell my heart was going through: work, a lot of work.

The drive was shorter than I anticipated, or perhaps my attention was simply elsewhere. I was surprised when we stopped in front of the manor's tall doors and Logan got out, pulling the driver's seat forward so I could contort my way out.

"Thanks," I muttered, taking his hand to disentangle myself from the backseat.

I couldn't look at him, but I needed to. As his partner on the Shifter Council, I had to. I had to see the dark glee in his eyes at my pain.

Pulling my gaze off the cobblestone driveway, I met his caramel depths. His hand still intertwined in my own, he gave a gentle squeeze. There was no joy at my misery, only compassion, and it threatened to break me all the more.

"I'm sorry, Olie," he said, gently and unexpectedly.

I nodded, unable to voice my thanks, choosing instead to storm into the house. I froze on the steps, however, staring at my SUV parked in the driveway. It was planned, he knew it was coming. Closing my eyes, I lost the fight as weakness dripped wetly down my face.

Grams greeted me at the threshold, uncertain and wary as I closed the oversized door quietly behind me. She wasn't the cause of my pain, not currently. I shouldn't take it out on her.

"I'll take those cases back now," I said softly, heading upstairs.

Her soft steps echoed behind me up the stairs and into her office, where I rummaged through her desk for the files.

"Are you certain that is a good idea?" She moved to my side, resting a hesitant hand on my shoulder.

"I am certain. Nothing good can come of my staying. At least on the road..." My voice cracked before I regained control. "On the road, no one will have to deal with my misery, and my anger will have an outlet."

She nodded, pulling her hand back while watching me closely.

"I'll have the rest of the files scanned over to you."

Why had I picked here for Grams's office? I asked my subconscious, which answered, probably because I didn't have a room here anymore. We were damn near at capacity and I had been staying at Blake's when in town.

I quickly turned away from those thoughts, accepting the file Grams handed to me, the one that I had been unable to find.

"He isn't worth it, Olie. You deserve better."

I didn't mean to laugh, but I couldn't help it. "I am a fool for believing anyone could ever love me."

"Oh, Olie," she said, reaching out again.

I pulled away, blinking back the sting of tears that just wouldn't fucking stop. "I have to go," I said, fleeing the safety of the manor.

I let the tears out along a deserted stretch of highway two hours out of town, sobbing until my throat felt raw and my stomach muscles hurt. Only a few headlights dotted this remote landscape as I made my way north to Pennsylvania. It would take me sixteen hours to make it there, to hunt down and kill a rogue vamp that had been taking out its nest mates.

Sixteen hours and then I could kill something. It couldn't happen soon enough.

Chapter 5

I drove straight through, only stopping for gas, water, and an occasional bathroom break. I ate once and it sat badly in my stomach. So, when I finally arrived at the small town of Wellsboro, I was primed to do some soul cleansing damage. Typically, I went to the source of the complaint first, asked a few questions and gathered some intel, but not today. Today caution could get lost.

Today, in the setting sun, I marched up to the dilapidated barn and threw open the rusted red door, sword in my hand.

"Come out and play, bitches," I taunted.

Several shadows moved rapidly over the rafters and I smiled. There was more than one.

...

I popped the trunk open and took out the baby wipes and a garbage bag. Those fuckers bled on *everything*. Stripping out of my now soiled black shirt, I used the wipes to clean my skin as best I could, along with the leather that wouldn't absorb the vile remnants of a vampire nest gone mad.

I heard the steps approaching me before he cleared this throat. I made no attempt to hurry my process. If he was here to try and kill me, I'd be pissed it was after I had cleaned up. Given his attempt to announce his presence, however, I was betting he wanted to talk about the vampire issue.

"Are you here to take care of the problem?" he asked uncertainly, coming around as I pulled a clean shirt on and tossed the bag of filth into the back.

"Problem is gone. Call whoever you reported this to and they'll come clean it up," I said, slamming the tailgate and making my way to the driver's door.

"You just got here," he argued, confused.

"I work fast," I called over my shoulder as I climbed into the SUV and started the engine. I called Grams.

"Olivia," she said on an exhale, clearly relieved I hadn't gotten myself killed.

"Wellsboro is done, next?"

Silence met my reply, but I waited. She knew me well. She understood I had to do this, it was the only thing left in my life that had meaning.

"Ohio looks to be the next in line," she rebounded. "I'm scanning over the report now." All business.

"Great." I answered, ending the call. Fucking Ohio. Again.

...

I zigged and zagged across my territory, killing anything and everything in my path. The calls from Kass, Jerry and even Darren had stopped coming and I was glad. I had nothing to say to any of them.

When Becky from security called me, however, I picked up on the first ring, curious and slightly worried.

"Hey Olie, I know you are busy but I want to run a few things by you," she began, chomping on her bubble gum.

"Go for it," I said, merging with traffic in Iowa.

"We've had three attempted break-ins at the Manor, all by vampires who, as far as I can tell, are unrelated to any of the Houses we have in town—" Becky tried to continue but I interrupted.

"Do you still have them?" I demanded.

"Yes, what do you want us to do with them? Torture has been unenlightening," she admitted, snapping her gum. "The only thing we've managed to find out is that they are here for Tate, but not in what capacity."

"Keep them for me," I answered, smiling.

"Done. Now, should we beef up security?"

I chewed on my lower lip, "No, if we are catching them, our security is working perfectly. And I want them to try again."

"Gotcha. ETA on your arrival?" she asked, idly clicking keys in the background. It felt good to be treated normally, not like the borderline psycho I admittedly was.

"Two days. I'm going to finish up this case and be back," I said, terminating the call.

Three vampires attempting to gain access into our compound, that didn't bode well for Tate at all.

...

It took me three days to get back, since the last beast I took down managed to take a chunk of my forearm with it. I needed a full day of sleep just so I could use it again.

Outside the Centennial Compound, I leaned against my car, debating if I should call first. Manners said I should, but my gut said I didn't give a flying fuck.

I left my weapons in the car. Just because I wanted to kill again, that didn't mean this was the place.

I sauntered up to the front door. The guards clearly remembered me, or perhaps it was the death that still clung to my clothing and hair. Either way, they called for Tate immediately.

"You need to wait here," a pleasant receptionist said, attempting to get me to sit after I passed the guards.

I scoffed, "Nice try, sweetie, where is Tate?"

Coming around her polished desk, she adjusted her formfitting suit. "I'm sorry, but he is in a meeting at the moment."

"Do you know who I am?" I asked, stepping toward her.

She swallowed loudly, showing she hadn't been a vamp for long. "Yes," she squeaked out.

"Do you know what I do?" I asked, leaning closer, my voice softening on the threat.

She nodded, properly terrified.

"Call Tate. NOW."

She scampered behind the desk, hitting buttons with trembling fingers.

"So now you pay us a visit," Mal said from behind me. I turned to see her arms crossed over her thin form, her auburn hair loose around her shoulders. With her designer clothing, she was regal in the opulent House.

I growled, "This isn't social."

"I heard," she said, turning away and motioning for me to follow her.

"Do you know anything about the attacks on the manor?" I asked her back, following her lead.

She stopped suddenly, turning back to me in shock. "Vampires are attacking the manor?"

"Yes, isn't that what you heard?" I asked her in annoyance. Patience was not a virtue I had ever acquired. Why didn't anyone understand that?

"No, I thought you were here about the wedding." She headed up the stairs to the second floor.

I shook my head. "Why would I care about a wedding?" I had certainly had my fill organizing Darren and Kass's, and there was still Logan and Lorraine's to come, which was on my to-do list. Far, far down the list.

Mal turned on the stairs. "Because Blake is getting married to Angelina."

I took a step back, shocked, as a million terrible emotions pumped through me. I tried my voice, but only a pathetic squeaking noise came out.

"Shit Olie, I thought you knew." She stepped closer.

I shook my head. "It doesn't matter." I forced my fingers to release the wood banister, on which they were leaving deep groove marks.

Mal touched my shoulder and I jerked back. I hadn't spent the last six weeks killing shit to let my emotions get the better of me now. I was a fucking Executioner first, and a person second.

"I think Blake is being forced into it," she offered.

"It's not my business." I forced a cold tone into my voice and eyes. How could this be happening? How little did I really mean to him? How pathetic that I was fooled so easily! My jaw tightened painfully.

Mal nodded slowly, cautiously stepping away from me before turning her back and heading back upstairs. I didn't think anyone was forcing Blake. I think he finally realized he was too good for me, and he was. There wasn't anything else to say on the score.

Finally off the stairs, we turned a corner and ran straight into Tate and Angelina.

"Olivia, I am not having this discussion with you," Tate sourly dismissed me, massaging his temples.

"Yes, you are." Please let him refuse me. Please let me have a reason to hurt him, anything.

"She isn't here about Blake," Mal enlightened him. "The manor has been attacked by rogue vampires as well."

"Dammit," Tate cursed. "This really isn't a good time for this."

"I don't give a fuck if this isn't an opportune time for you, Tate. I want information on why vampires are attacking my home," I challenged him, wishing I had my weapons on me.

"That isn't my fault," he snarled back.

I searched his eyes. "Liar."

He lunged at me and I smiled, glad to have rattled him. Unfortunately, Mal grabbed his hand at the last second and pulled him back, rendering both of them off balance. Seething, he regarded me for a long moment before muttering, "I will take care of it."

"See that you do," I said to his back.

While the Manor had a beautiful gym, not to mention the dance rooms used by the Kitten dancers, I just wasn't in the mood. Instead, I stormed out of the Centennial House and pulled into Sonny's Boxing Gym, a local joint owned by a shifter I had met during my arbitrating with Logan.

I needed to work off some steam on a punching bag or a shifter. I wasn't particular.

As I entered the musty gym, the high ceiling fans working overtime to spread the cool air around, heads turned. I surveyed the place with my bag slung over my shoulder. I wasn't working out in my leathers.

Alec, a powerful wolf shifter and Logan's right hand man, jogged over, sweat dripping from his auburn locks, "You need me?"

We had developed a friendship based on beating the shit out people.

"Only if you want your ass beat," I advised, smiling. "I need to work out some tension."

Alec smiled good-naturedly. "Let me show you to the locker rooms."

"Thanks," I answered, trying to ignore the stares.

"Don't see many females in here," he offered, holding open the women's locker room door for me.

"That was apparent."

"I'm at the bags when you are ready."

I took my time, splashing cold water on my face and re-wrapping my raw forearm. I frowned at the wound that my natural healing would knit together faster if I rested and took better care of myself. I didn't. The pain was a sensation I enjoyed.

Dressed in a sports bra and yoga pants, I went out in search of wraps and gloves.

Sonny found his way over to me, puffing on a cigar and holding out pink wraps and gloves while arguing with someone on the phone. I took the offering, smiling my thanks, and headed toward the bags and Alec.

He stopped his assault on the bag, reaching a hand out to steady its sway. "Fuck, Olivia, what happened to you?" he asked, taking a once-over of my body.

I shrugged. "Work."

"Then work is beating the shit out of you." His eyes roved over my wrapped forearm and bruised ribs.

"I can put a shirt on if some combat wounds bother you," I snipped.

Alec held his hands out for the wraps, his face carefully neutral. "You do need to work out some tension. What's up?" He started wrapping the pink material on my left hand.

"Vamps are attacking the manor," I confessed.

"Local?"

"Don't appear to be," I answered, as he moved to the other hand.

"What are you going to do?" he asked, taking a surreptitious glance at my clenched jaw.

"Find the nest and deliver their heads on spikes."

To Alec's credit, he didn't pause at my gruesome description or correct me that vampire heads couldn't be put on spikes, since they turned to dust.

Smart man.

"You know what you are doing?" he asked.

I rolled my eyes and attacked the bag with all the anger and frustration that Blake's wedding announcement had instilled in me, not to mention the fight with Grams or the fucking vampires attacking what I cherished most.

Sweat dripped into my eyes and my raw forearm burned with exhaustion from attacking the bag with more energy than I had anticipated.

When my arms shook from exertion I stopped, leaning my forehead against the bag, feeling the stitching, sucking down sweet air. "Thanks, Alec," I said to his wide eyes. "I needed that."

"I guess," he said, releasing the bag to crack his knuckles. "Tyler is looking for a partner in the ring if you are up to it. He's a mean son of a bitch, though."

I smiled as I headed to the drinking fountain. "Sounds like fun."

Cheers went up from the ring—thanks to shifter hearing, nothing was private. I splashed cool water on my face and turned to walk over to the giant of a man. I ignored the stares of those who had stopped their workouts to watch. He was larger than Alec; where Alec had trained for lean muscle that made him deadly quick, Tyler had stocky muscle upon muscle. Idly, I wondered what animal he shifted into.

I couldn't help my smile. This was going to be fun. I was still fucking irritated.

Sonny came up from behind me, halting my progress toward Tyler. He outfitted me with headgear and a mouthpiece, the cigar still dangling from his lips. I watched Tyler bounce energetically from foot to foot, loudly boasting.

"You sure you can handle all this, little girl?" he taunted.

I smiled and nodded, speech hindered by the mouthpiece. I was certain my eyes conveyed my excitement.

After securing the chinstrap a little too tightly, Sonny held me at arm's length. "Do not kill him," he warned, his dark eyes serious.

I nodded, patting him on the shoulder with a gloved hand.

"My ulcers can't take this," he grunted, moving out of my way.

I slipped into the ring gracefully, keeping my attention on Tyler the entire time.

He hadn't opted for headgear or a mouthpiece. I shrugged. Dental work was expensive and took time I didn't have.

As we touched gloves in the center of the ring, I watched his posture, knowing by the bunching of his thigh muscles that he would charge me as soon as the bell rang.

The metal bell announced our fight with a shrill peal. I felt the others watching us, gathered around the ring, but my gaze was only for Tyler. Here's hoping he could handle me.

Just as predicted, he came out of his corner with his center of mass lowered as he tried to bowl me over. I dodged easily enough, resting my weight on the balls of my feet.

He turned, letting his right hand swing with a force I couldn't help but admire. I definitely could not let those shots connect with my face. I would go down hard and not come back up, protective headgear or not. Ducking under his attempts, I twisted around him, changing our positions.

I should have clarified beforehand whether this was strictly a boxing match, or if I was allowed to add wrestling in as well.

Oh well, I would just play off of what Tyler did. Currently he was trash talking me, but I wasn't listening to him or the cheers from the spectators crowded around us.

My focus narrowed to his arms and his pretty thick-skulled head, which he didn't cover up nearly well enough.

I didn't wait for him to finish the sentence about him being the recipient of a kiss when he was finished kicking my ass. I rushed him, closing the distance with quick strides before I landed two hooks to each side of his head.

Dazed, he stumbled back as I followed up with three swift uppercuts to his stomach. He doubled over, looking up at me with the change present in his eyes.

"Go ahead, bitch," I taunted. Bringing a little shifter action into the ring would make this more of a challenge.

His upper body rippled and grew. Shouts of foul reached my ears for his partially shifting, but I didn't care. He charged me like a buffalo, aiming his shoulder toward my midsection again. I wasn't as fast in dodging him this time. I went down to all fours and he tripped over me, landing in the ropes awkwardly.

Smiling around the mouth guard, I pushed up from the stiff mat, waving him to try again.

He was faster than I expected, his charge landing against my midsection, pushing me back into the ropes.

I gasped for breath and found any effort futile; I was equally unable to push or punch him. Instead, I drew my feet up and slammed my heels against his sternum, giving myself enough room to crash to the mat and roll away. Springing up behind him, I sucked in air as he turned, throwing jabs at my face again.

I ducked quickly, shuffling back, looking for an opportunity. It came in the form of his unbalance as he put everything he had into his last jab that connected with my shoulder. I moved in closer and took him down to the mat with a kick to the knee.

Straddling him, I blasted his face with punch after punch, hearing the satisfying crunch of his breaking nose, several times. His quick healing was annoying me.

It was a satisfying beat-down to deliver, but it wasn't enough to knock him out. He launched me away from him, his hands on my shoulders as he used his momentum to shove me. I flew out of the ring, tucking and rolling against the hard concrete, feeling my shoulder take the brunt of the impact painfully.

A small whimper escaped my lips. I lay exactly how I had fallen, holding my stomach and braiding down the pain, a trick I'd long coveted and now was teaching to other succubi like me. When our emotions are too raw, too powerful, it helps to imagine the sensations as corded rope. From there the concept of braiding is easy, the mental exercise keeping us from inadvertently influencing entire rooms.

Slowly, I sat up, pain throbbing in time with my heart. Tyler reached me first, panic in his eyes.

"Shit, I am so sorry," he said, taking off my headgear with rough movements. I spat my mouthpiece out, grinding my jaw together.

"Dammit to hell!" Sonny yelled. "My insurance can't handle this!" He rushed up, first aid kit in tow.

"Relax, I don't think it's broken," I hissed.

"Olivia!" I heard my name being screamed out of more than one mouth.

"What?" I groaned out, peering up through squinted eyes at Kass, Darren and Logan. How did they know where to find me?

Logan reached me first. He removed his coat mid-stride, draping it over a bench press before he squatted behind me. He rested his hands lightly on my waist, heat from the touch seeping throughout my exposed torso.

"Alec, check it," he commanded.

"Don't hit me," Alec instructed me, settling to his knees on the concrete in front of me.

"No promises," I groaned out. He pressed his warm hands into the tender flesh of my abused shoulder.

Over his shoulder I saw Tyler, eyes wide, sweating profusely, worry etched in the lines of his forehead.

My back arched, my body wanting away from the pain he was inflicting. A scream firmly trapped between my lips, I couldn't stop my head lolling back onto Logan's shoulder.

"Almost done, Olie," Alec comforted, pulling on my wrist quickly while applying pressure to my dislocated shoulder.

I sucked in air, ready to launch at him, but thankfully Logan's hands tightened on my hips, pinning me in place. I exhaled in a pained whoosh.

"You need to ice that." Alec stood, easing my weight up as well, careful to steady me.

"Alpha, I am so sorry. We were just screwing around," Tyler rapidly explained. He was clearly not sure whom to be more afraid of, me or Logan.

"It's fine, Tyler," I groaned.

Kass elbowed her way to the front, "Why are you here, Olie?" Her sharp gaze didn't miss my underweight form. The hurt from my ignoring her was evident.

I sighed, seeing no use in dragging the announcement out. "Blake is getting married."

"Oh." She looked as shocked and confused as I felt.

"I thought you guys were an item?" Alec asked, handing me a towel.

I shook my head, "Nope."

"Oh," Alec said, copying Kass as he looked me over again, or rather, checked me out this time.

"Don't get any ideas," I growled. "I am still unstable."

Alec smiled and gave an almost bashful shrug. Logan growled behind me.

I figured I might as well shift my annoyance to someone who deserved it. "What are you doing here, Logan?"

"You get cleaned up, let's grab lunch." He obviously ignored my question, also noticing my recent weight loss.

I shrugged, heading towards the locker room. Kass was right behind me. She was upset, to put it mildly.

I waited until I was in the shower and couldn't see her to ask, "What's wrong?"

"He's getting married? Already?" she screeched, giving my thoughts a voice, having finally processed the information.

"Yep." I didn't want to dwell on it.

"Do you think he was seeing her the whole time?" she asked. Her annoyance had shifted from my avoidance to him, thankfully.

"I hope not." I hadn't dreamed of that possibility.

"Shit Olie, he is such an asshole!" She stomped her foot for emphasis.

"It doesn't matter what he does now, Kass. We are done and over," I told her, or was I telling myself? I wasn't telling her Mal thought it was forced. That would give her hope, and that was the last thing I needed. Hope was dangerous.

"I guess."

"How are you feeling?" I needed a topic change.

She groaned, "Like shit."

I couldn't help but laugh.

"I missed you, Olie." Her voice was earnest and I paused in the shower.

"I know, Kass, I just—I just had to get away for a while."

"I know," she answered sadly.

I came out of the shower dressed in a tank top and a clean pair of jeans. I hated that I was the reason for the tears in her eyes.

"Shut up. It's the hormones," she claimed.

"Okay." I pulled her in for a hug, ignoring the real reason.

...

Logan had an ice pack waiting when we exited the locker room.

"I'll see you both at the restaurant," Kass stated, taking Darren's hand and heading outside.

Logan strapped the pack to my shoulder over my tank top with a practiced ease. His hands lingered longer than they should have, his warm touch stirring a lonely misery I wanted nothing to do with. He guided my arm to rest against my waist and his gaze fell on my injured wrist. Shaking his head, he said, "You love trouble."

I shrugged. "I ducked when I should have shot."

He finished wrapping the gauze around my forearm, smoothing the edges of the bandage. Looking down at me with a mixture of irritation and interest, he pulled my bag over his shoulder.

"Let me drive," he asked, or maybe commanded. Either way I liked being driven around so I handed over the keys.

"You know where we are going?" I questioned, waving to Kass as we exited into the midday sun.

"Yep," he answered.

I yawned, "Lead on, I'm starved."

...

Someone had clearly relayed my passion for pizza. As we spread out around a circular table in a pizzeria that smelled divine, I inhaled deeply, moaning.

"When was the last time you ate, Olie?" Kass was trying for nonchalance, but her worried tone wasn't lost on me.

I shrugged. "Honestly, I don't remember."

"You look thinner," Logan commented, putting the menu down.

"I've been busy. But enough about me, why are you three hunting me down?"

Logan shifted in his chair and Kass stared daggers at him. "Actually, Kass, why don't you tell me," I amended. "It'll be so much faster."

"Lorraine is spending Logan into debt." Her disgust was plain.

"How did she get access to his money?" I asked, picking up a piece of bread the server delivered. We interrupted our conversation to order.

Logan cleared his throat, "She is handling my personal finances, so I can focus on the shifters properly."

"Handling you into bankruptcy." I laughed at my own joke.

He didn't share my mirth, so I went on. "How many personal bills could you possibly have, anyways?" Grams handled all of my finances.

"A lot," he informed me cryptically.

Rolling my eyes, I turned to Kass with a shrug. "I'm okay with him being poor."

Kass huffed, "He is borrowing from us. Darren just started his new personal security business and Logan's incompetence is making my life fucking miserable."

Darren rubbed the bridge of his nose and Logan said nothing. The fact that they were brothers was undeniable. In addition to the strong set of their jaws and the natural tan I was so jealous of, they also carried themselves with an unmistakable confidence—although in Logan's case, I like to call it his asshole-ness.

"Why can't Kass do your books? You handle Darren's at home, right?" I suggested.

Kass narrowed her eyes at me. "I do."

"And you are managing to avoid bankruptcy," I confirmed.

"We are doing just fine," her eyes narrowed further.

"I like it," Logan said stuffing his face with bread.

"Why do I have to babysit his poor decisions?" she groaned, annoyed.

"I've been asking myself that a lot, and the only answer I come up with is because you married Darren." I shrugged. I had at least made my peace with the fact the shifters' future and my own were now firmly intertwined.

"Ugh, so true. You were never so involved in the shifter sphere." She rubbed the back of her neck, shifting in the chair uncomfortably with her growing belly.

I licked my lips greedily as our food was delivered.

"Have you seen Jerry?" I asked, biting down into the greasy cheese pizza.

Kass nodded, casting a sidelong look at Darren. "He and Mark are having problems."

"That sucks," I said. "I need to talk to him about the witches. Those crazy assholes are practicing all over my territory."

"What are they doing?" Logan asked.

"Nothing too out of the ordinary, from what I know. It's just been some time since I've stumbled across their circle with blood sacrifices. Granted, it was a goat and a chicken, but my gut tells me there's something behind it I'm not going to like."

"Have you talked to Garrick?" Kass asked, changing the subject away from sacrifices while we ate.

I shifted, uncomfortably.

"You haven't forgotten about the upcoming meetings?" she pressed.

I groaned, "No, I have not forgotten about The Conferences or who will be there." The Conferences was the largest gathering of Supernaturals in the world. This year it was being held stateside and saving me a fortune on plane tickets.

I had to go. It was part of the job and one of the duties assigned to me.

"It's just a breeding ground for drama and fights," I groaned, snagging the last slice of pizza off the pan.

Logan grunted and I chose to take that as agreement. "It's a necessary evil."

"Are you going?" I asked Kass.

Darren answered, placing a hand protectively on her stomach, "No."

Kass gave him an annoyed glare. "I can answer for myself."

Darren shrugged, returning to his meal. "I can't help it. You and the baby are throwing all my protective instincts into overdrive."

"Aww," I teased, laughing when Kass leveled her glare at me. "Don't worry, Darren, I wouldn't have let her go, either."

"Seriously, do I have no free will, you fucking assholes?" She slammed her drink down.

"Yes," I answered, figuring I was better suited to take the heat than Darren, "but you are ours to protect and taking you to The Conferences is dangerous. Just be happy Darren doesn't cut up your food."

Darren smiled at Kass. "He tried," she answered blandly.

"It's all from a place of love," I assured her.

She huffed, ignoring me good-naturedly to pick up eating again.

"Who is Garrick?" Logan asked, munching on his meat lovers pizza.

"He's a vampire who runs the western territory, my counterpart on the Supernatural Council. I would have thought you'd met him, being leader of the entire U.S."

Logan thought about that. Casting a look at Darren, he cleared his throat. "The alphas of the western US deal with things themselves, they don't subcontract with the Council like we do here."

I nodded. "Interesting. I wonder if he knows the revenue stream he is missing."

"You two actually get along?" Logan asked.

Kass choked on her water. I smiled, "It's a complicated relationship."

Kass snorted, "Last time you two were in the same room, it had to be evacuated."

"We made up." In his bedroom, several times over. "To answer the question, Garrick leaves me alone and I leave him alone. The only time we see each other is at The Conferences. We handle our situations differently. He's much better at politics than I am."

Logan chuckled, "That isn't a great feat."

"True," I admitted, leaning back in my chair. "What are we getting for dessert?"

Thinking of Garrick had my mind shifting back to Blake and all the things I wished I could forget.

"I'm thinking at least one of each," Kass purred, looking over the dessert menu propped on the table.

"I like the way you think."

Chapter 6

Kass had been right. Mark and Jerry were having serious issues.

Logan went with Kass and Darren after lunch and I headed over to the historical district close to downtown. I hadn't thought to call ahead. I probably should have.

I had stopped mid-knock, waiting outside on their porch, listening to the slamming and the yelling. I could feel the anger, fear, and pain radiating from the house. I was debating coming back later when the door flew open and Mark fled the scene. If he saw me, it didn't slow his progress.

I waited off to the side of the open door, expecting Jerry to run after him. I think Mark did as well, as he stared at the open door from his car, with misty eyes and labored breaths. Slamming a hand against the steering wheel, he threw the vehicle into reverse and fled the quaint house they shared together.

Blowing out a breath, I secured my own emotions behind thick barriers before crossing the threshold uninvited.

"Go away," Jerry groaned, standing at the cart bar and pouring himself a drink. His bloodshot eyes took a moment to focus on the fact it was me and not Mark.

"Wanna talk about it?" I asked, closing the door softly behind me. His eyes followed the door painfully until it clicked shut.

"No," Jerry whispered, his dark skin a contrast to the cream sofa he fell onto.

He no longer resembled the carefree youth I had met not too long ago. Before me now was a weary soul who, like me, had done and seen too much. The scars left behind didn't leave much room for the love of a good partner, like Mark.

Even if we were both trying—well, he was trying. I was trying to forget.

"What do you want?" he asked, dragging his bloodshot eyes to my own.

I sat at the edge of the sofa, facing him. "The witches are up to something."

He scoffed, standing and throwing his glass in the same movement. It shattered against the far wall. The effort threw him off balance. "I don't KNOW ANYTHING, Olivia. Why are you here?" He rounded on me, bellowing, "Why can't you go kill something, torture someone, to get your information? Why do I have to be your liaison to the witches because your piss poor manners and 'poor me' excuses grant you leave to do anything you want?" He moved to make another drink, stumbling. "Oh right, I forgot, your boyfriend—" heavy emphasis of, "*left you*. He finally realized you were more trouble than a fuck was worth."

I was aware he wasn't really angry at me, but the digs stung, anyway. In that moment, hurting him would have felt wonderful. Clenching my jaw, I stood. I really wanted to tell him where to shove it, but I wasn't risking the tears that would make me weak, so instead I just turned and left.

He called after me, "Shit, Olie, I'm sorry. Mark wants to adopt a shifter and I—" I closed the door on his words, exhaling a ragged breath.

I'd forgive him, but not today.

I slammed the door of my SUV and called Becky. My fingers clenched the steering wheel with deadly force.

"Yo boss," she greeted me, chomping on something probably high in sugar.

"Prep the trespassers. I'll be there in thirty."

I could hear the grin in her answer, "Yes ma'm."

...

I don't typically keep prisoners. But when a space was needed for interrogation in the short term, we had an old farmhouse outfitted with soundproof rooms and all the toys a girl like me could ask for.

I had both vampires strung up by their wrists, toes brushing the old concrete flooring. Running my fingers over cold metal blades of various sizes, I hummed soothingly to myself. The third one had died shortly after I arrived in town.

Having made my decision, I sat down in front of them on the tacky vinyl chair liberated from the ramshackle farmhouse kitchen.

"So, who would like to speak first?" I asked, pointing the blade between the two of them.

Stiff shoulders and clenched jaws met my request, eyes riveted behind me.

I sighed happily. "I was really hoping you'd say that."

...

Six hours later, both the vampires were dead. I had wanted to prolong their demise to send a message, but I had things to do.

"I got nothing, boss," Becky informed me through the cell phone clamped tightly to my ear. I hated when she called me that. I had flashbacks of that horrible strip club I had been forced to infiltrate.

"Dammit," I hissed, listening to her chomp her gum.

"You do the boys dirty?" she asked eagerly.

I stifled a laugh, looking around at the dust on the floor.

"You would have been proud."

She sighed, "I always miss the good ones."

"Next time I'll show more restraint," I promised. I felt better having mutilated the two vampires but Jerry's words still stung in my raw wounds.

"I'll try Mal." Not that she wanted to hear from me. "Thanks, Becky. "

"Anytime, boss."

I cleaned up my mess, my mind occupied as I completed the menial task before heading down to the kitchen. There I washed my hands under the cold water and dried them on the paper towels.

Satisfied that my mess was cleaned up, I set the alarm and locked the doors before stomping down the faded white steps and into my SUV.

I texted Mal my request and fiddled with the radio while I waited for her to respond.

I needed her to run the names that the now deceased informants had given me. I had spent the night toying around with boys and though it would be bedtime for Mal, I was hoping to catch her before she turned in.

Fine, hurry up, she responded to my text.

I smiled, pocketing my phone and heading out.

...

A grumpy Mal met me at the front door. Apparently, I caused too many problems on my own. Silently, we made our way to their computer lab.

"What do you have on Patricia Bellarosa?" I asked, sitting in a chair next to her and looking over her shoulder. It was just she and I here at this early hour.

"What do you want with her?" she grumbled as she typed rapidly, still annoyed that I was keeping her from her beauty sleep.

Tommy, my usual hacker and computer guru, was on a group vacation to Disneyland. I missed him dearly. I did not want to be here.

Resting my chin in my palm, I watched the screen pull up a beautiful woman with long ice-blond hair and a cruel smile.

"Wow," Mal whistled. "Every House that took her in exiled her. That takes talent."

I grunted in agreement. She was just under a hundred years old and, from the information listed about her, as twisted as they came. There was even a mention of her draining babies.

"Why hasn't anyone put her down?" I asked, both disgusted with the file and annoyed that the vampires hadn't taken care of their dirty laundry, especially after they'd come out of the proverbial closet and announced themselves to the humans.

"They've tried, it wasn't successful. She's a killer for hire now and her record is impressive."

"Not as impressive as mine."

"Is this what you need?"

"No." Rubbing my tired eyes, I searched the screen again, trying to see a connection between her and Tate.

Mal's phone pinged at her and she sighed heavily. "I gotta go, security issue."

I nodded, still staring at the screen.

"Let yourself out and do not start trouble."

I nodded absentmindedly, not hearing the door shut behind her. What was I missing? Tate had never taken her in and there was no mention of them being at the same Houses. Maybe they met somewhere? The name would ring a bell? Maybe this was all a wild goose chase. I didn't even know if this name was real or a trumped up lead to keep me spinning in circles. I needed to find the bitch and have a conversation, one killer to another.

Leaning back in my chair, I closed my eyes, mentally ticking off my to-do list: I had to find Patricia Bellarosa. I needed the witches to stop whatever weird shit they were up to. And I'd better patch up my rocky relationship with Grams, not to mention my damaged relationship with Jerry. The list felt endless, my burdens had never felt this heavy before. My life was divided into two categories, before and after Blake. Damn my weak heart for missing him so.

Rubbing my temples, I heard the door open. "Forgot something?" I asked Mal.

Silence met my answer. I looked over to ask her if I needed an escort out. The words died on my lips, my mouth hanging open as Blake stood over me, staring down from impossibly blue eyes.

51

Shock and desire removed the air in my lungs. Pain followed shortly after and had me launching out of my seat, backing away from him, stumbling over my upturned chair. My miserable body responded to him in ways I didn't need him scenting.

His inhale and upturned lips told me it was too late.

Shit.

"Olivia." My name on his lips was almost too much. I couldn't look at him, shame forcing me to look away. I had shown him all my broken pieces, he knew too much.

He stepped closer, between my car keys and me.

SHIT.

I couldn't look at him, shouldn't look at him. Another look into those devastatingly handsome eyes and I'd give in to my desires.

I was certain of it.

Just to feel him near again, to hear my name on his lips in pleasure, to be chosen over Angelina.

I wanted to be worthy of his love.

His gentle touch under my chin had me gasping for air, the contact jarring me to my toes. I looked into his mesmerizing cobalt gaze.

"Find what you are looking for?" His soft voice washed over me, heat pooling inside of me.

"No." My voice was hardly above a whisper. My eyes searched his, wanting, needing to understand this sudden change in him. Hope, that foolish beast, was willing him to have changed his mind. Clan be dammed.

Damn him and that slow seductive smile.

Damn my traitorous body.

I had to get back in control. I had to push his advancing form away. I couldn't let his lips come any closer to my own.

I shouldn't want this, he broke my heart and he didn't get a second chance.

But I'd do anything just to have him back, just to feel whole for a little while longer.

"Blake," I whispered before his lips grazed mine.

Thoughts fled me, instinct and need dominated.

He nuzzled the sensitive flesh under my ear, my hands fisting into his shirt of their own will, closing the distance between our bodies.

The emotional distance dissipated, followed by my pants. The ripping sound must have been my underwear. His hands on my ass lifted me up to be impaled on his waiting length. Our lips still intertwined, I squealed into his mouth, a dark chuckle answering my cry.

Something hard hit my back and I assumed it was the wall. I was all sensation, the pain in my chest easing, the joy of being reconnected to him forcing tears to leak down my cheeks.

My soul was home.

I panted, holding onto him as the pleasure stole feeling in my limbs. Closing my eyes and nuzzling my face into his neck, I exhaled, feeling everything inside me settle into perfection.

"Shit," he whispered suddenly, pulling back to look down at me. I looked up, and regret looked back at me.

"What's wrong?" I asked as he pulled out of me, dropping my legs abruptly. Thankfully, they held, shaky as I was.

As he put himself together quickly I could only stare at him in confusion, but he wouldn't meet my gaze.

"I can't be with you, Olivia." He came closer, still avoiding my gaze, but resting a hand against my heart.

"I love you, but I can't do this."

His words emptied my heart of my short-lived joy and I gave serious thought to killing him.

If I thought for a second it would end the pain inside of me, I would have.

I pulled on jeans, leaving my ruined underwear behind, and leaving the compound with a promise I would never return.

...

I didn't run to my SUV, but I wanted to like in one of those terribly cheesy romance movies Kass forced me to watch. My heart shattered and with every step, the pieces crunched under foot.

Instead, I left just how I had entered, silently, my posture stiff and my emotions under heavy guard.

I didn't remember the drive, didn't recall getting out of the SUV and falling to my knees at Lawrence's grave, but here I was again, seeking comfort from Logan and Darren's grandfather. Stephen, the Puppet Master, had reanimated him, bringing my life info full frontal contact with the shifters.

Rubbing a hand over my face, I leaned against the cold stone, wiling my heart to grow cold as well, but my damn brain wouldn't shut off. Blake's final words were on repeat inside my head: I love you, but I can't do this.

Chapter 7

My phone ringing relentlessly finally pulled me from my despondent stupor.

I glared at the screen. "What?" I muttered to Logan.

"You are needed," he said, his words clipped in anger. "NOW."

I looked at the screen, seeing that he had hung up on me. I couldn't bring myself to care.

Sure would be nice to know *where* I was needed.

I pushed myself up and worked the kinks out on my way back to the SUV.

Kass called next, sobbing, "Olie, where are you?"

"On my way." So that's where I was needed.

...

I parked in front of Darren and Kass's home. It was in a newly built neighborhood with pristine landscaping and green shaded parks. Before rising from the driver's seat, I had to take a moment to center my emotions as best as I could.

This distraction helped, but my misery was still threatening to crush me.

Blowing out a breath, I opened the SUV's door, then slammed it loudly behind me before striding to the front door. Logan yanked it open before I could even knock. He took a deep breath as I walked by, a soft chuckle on his lips.

"So soon?" he questioned, irritated, why I have no idea. Who I slept with wasn't any of his business.

I turned, my blood running cold. He smelled Blake on me. For one painful moment my guards broke, pain lacing my heart and trying to push tears from my eyes.

Anger fast followed. "Leave it," I warned him.

Voices in the kitchen drew me.

"This is not up for debate," Kass hissed at Darren, her mocha eyes narrowed at him, a half-eaten cookie dangling forgotten in her fingers. She must be pissed.

Darren tried not to back away from the venom in her stare, but his jaw tightened as he watched her. "I do not need a babysitter."

Kass threw up her hands, the cookie spraying crumbs and her anger rapidly switching to tears. "This isn't about you! This is about the fact that every female shifter has been throwing herself at you, even when I am present!" Her face fell as her voice broke. "Olivia can keep them off you better than I can, just please take her."

I wasn't sure if it was the tears or the pleading that did it, but I watched Darren reach out and fold her into his arms, "Okay, okay," he whispered.

Hannah looked at me with a raised eyebrow, "Yeah, you keep them harlots off my Daddy."

I smiled, patting her head, "As you command."

"Who taught you that word?" Kass asked, coming in with Darren to the living room.

"Olie," Hannah stated proudly.

I ducked my head, with a small grin.

"I'll deal with you later," she informed me. "In the meantime, do what the kid says."

I smiled at them; I needed a good fight.

...

We met Lorraine, Logan and Alec outside in the dusty parking lot of The Were. It was a local bar for shifters and shifters only, a place to indulge their primal instincts of fighting and fucking. Judging from the grunts and groans in the dark parking lot, not to mention the lust and desire seeping from the cracked wood, it was more the latter.

We had driven separately to the seedy establishment so Logan could get the pain in the ass fiancée and his own security. I felt right at home. I hadn't wanted details of their meeting, even though they were offered. I honestly couldn't bring myself to care.

As we headed toward the front door, a group of smokers loitering on the open porch, dressed in cut off tops, leather skirts, and tight jeans, watched our approach with clear interest. I surveyed the group, hoping for trouble.

I inhaled deeply. This was just the release I needed.

Lorraine stalked to the other side of Logan, her heels getting caught in the holes in the parking lot.

"What a loathsome establishment," she hissed at him.

I rolled my eyes and shared a look with Darren. Every shifter here had just heard her. Well, perhaps not those inside the club, given the thumping music, but it was still an ignorant statement to make while engaged to the Alpha of the Shifter Nation. The music was far quieter than in a normal club, in deference to the shifters' superb hearing, but even they enjoyed drowning their gifted senses in the pulsating beat.

Darren blew out a breath. "This is an interesting choice of venue," he muttered to Logan, fully knowing his voice would carry.

Logan only shrugged, practically carrying Lorraine. "He's difficult to deal with; giving him home field advantage will hopefully help smooth things over." I smiled, happy Logan was setting a precedent that didn't require me to behave.

Darren huffed. I stayed out of it. I was not here tonight in my official capacity as right-hand arbitrator for Logan. I was only here to make sure no one grabbed, molested, or harassed Darren.

Easy peasy.

The bouncer at the front door gave me a long look when it was my turn to gain entrance. The tall, tattooed man inhaled deeply. "Not a shifter," he growled.

I slid up into his personal space. "Wanna take a guess?" I whispered sultrily.

Tall and beefy's head dipped over my body in appreciation before his eyes settled on my own, a wisp of a smile on his lips.

"She's with us," Alec said, dragging me away from him.

"Wait!" The bouncer called out, his brain cells firing again. "She needs to be searched."

I pulled out of Alec's hand as Logan and Darren looked worriedly back at me. Turning, I held my hands out as the bouncer reached out to pat my arms. I let my power out, desire seeping into his hands. Raw, potent need flowed under his skin as his hands checked my hips.

He inhaled a shaky breath, hands running over my spread thighs. He missed the knives in my boots, standing back up, breathing heavily. I turned with a smile back to my group.

I was going to have fun tonight.

The interior of the club was everything I had expected: low lighting for the shifters' excellent eyesight, a deep bass pulsing through the strategically placed speakers, and the scent of wet, sweaty dog. I'd never admit that last observation unless I was looking for a fight.

Actually, I might be.

Logan and Darren were escorted to a round booth near the back, next to the bar. Alec and I stayed standing, surveying the scene as the other three settled with a new member of the group. My gut had me instantly disliking him and I wasn't sure if it was the slimy appearance of his hair or the grainy cast to his skin. I was certain that the cagey, drunk eyes roving over my body had more to do with it.

I adjusted my stance, watching his hands closely. Shifters having a drink was not an uncommon event, but a drunk shifter was something else. That took talent, to overload their hyperactive metabolisms to achieve a state of inebriation.

I tuned out the conversation at the table, choosing to focus on the bar instead. A long haired beauty with a deep tan, dark makeup, and an alluring smile moved quickly filling drink orders, her movements sure and practiced as she delivered alcohol to the waiting crowds. The darkly lit dance floor was loosely populated with couples wrapped delectably around each other, pelvises aligned and grinding with a single-minded need.

I was jealous of their total abandonment of rational thought.

Turning my attention back in front of me, I raised an eyebrow at Alec who was sipping a beer. "How did you get served so quickly?" I asked him softly.

He smiled and flexed. I couldn't help but roll my eyes. I turned my attention to Lorraine, sandwiched between the larger men, looking miserable. That brought an honest grin to my face.

A woman's sweaty body pressed again my own. "Darren!" she called out, trying to move me.

I shoved back hard, moving her back a few steps.

"What the fuck, bitch?" she hissed, apparently now just seeing me.

Tilting my head, I took in her small shorts and leather bra, crossing my arms over my chest.

"What do you want?" I asked.

"You need to move, little girl, before I break you. Darren needs to speak with me," she claimed, throwing her long hair back.

"Why?" I asked, unimpressed.

She scoffed, unable to come up with an intelligent answer. "Because I said so."

"Worshiping, pawing and/or fawning over Darren is officially closed. Find someone else," I told her, turning my attention elsewhere as I dismissed her.

Her chest heaved, hands clenched at her side. Alec was still watching her and I saw the exact moment he opened his mouth to warn me about her approach. Still sporting a small smile, I kept eye contact with him as I captured her arm. Her closed fist, swinging toward my jaw, twisted at an unnatural angle. The solid snap of her elbow breaking brought me joy.

She cried out. Alec's mouth hung open in disbelief as I used my body weight to drop her down to her knees. I didn't release her arm, which would allow the bone to heal.

"Are you done?" I asked softly.

"Yes," she whimpered, gasping for breath, tears leaking down her painted cheeks.

I pushed her away from me, standing back to my full height. She used her feet to push back away from me, not daring to challenge me again with direct eye contact. If she had a tail it would have been tucked.

A slow clap coming from the dance floor behind me had my attention as I readied for another attack. I was pleasantly surprised to see Bear, right at home with his thick tattooed arms and shaved head.

"Olivia, I see you have introduced yourself," he commented, standing close. I inhaled the smell of beer and the wild woods. I liked the heat from his body and the close proximity.

I grunted a noncommittal response, scowling.

He smiled. Seriously, when did I get less threatening?

He leaned into my personal space, peering at me inquisitively. I asked, "What?"

"I hear you're a single lady now."

I raised an eyebrow at him, looking at him with new eyes. Bear was undoubtedly an attractive man, with his shaved head and tightly defined muscles. I chewed on my bottom lip thoughtfully, my gaze roving over hard-packed muscle. My attention did not go unnoticed. He smiled, leaning closer.

"Oh, for—seriously? Keep it in your damn pants," Lorraine spat, interrupting our moment.

"I couldn't have said it better myself," Logan warned quietly.

"Shut it." I pointed at him.

"The demon whore is free to whore once again." Lorraine lifted her drink in salute.

"At least I'm in demand."

"Enough," Darren commanded.

Shit, he was right. I was letting my temper and pain get the best of me. I was not presenting a very professional image for the shifters as one holding a place of honor next to Logan. I glared daggers at Lorraine, wishing I could reach out and shove the aforementioned daggers where the sun didn't shine.

My phone vibrating ceased our conversation. With a sigh I picked up.

"Hi Grams."

"Olivia, we have a problem."

Biting down the groan I asked, "What kind of a problem?" So fucking help me if Tommy got himself kidnapped again.

"I think it's best if you see for yourself, I'm emailing the pictures over now. Oh, and do be sure to bring Jerry along. This has the particular stench of those wretched witches."

The click ending our conversation had me biting down on my words. Jerry. Uh, pretty sure I didn't want to talk to him yet.

I looked back to Logan and Darren, who were both staring at me.

"Hurry the fuck up. I have business to attend to."

Tactful, that's my middle name.

...

I was back in front of Jerry's house and Mark's vehicle was still absent. I was hoping that he was just at work or busy and not still gone from the fight I had witnessed. I was fairly certain that was at least a day ago. I still hadn't stopped to sleep. It seemed less important now that I was doing it alone.

Grunting, I flung the car door open into the dark street. I marched heavily toward the door, prepared to drag him out of his house if necessary.

He opened it before I got there. I stopped halfway through the front yard.

We regarded each other for a moment.

"Come in, Olie," he spoke first, moving back to allow me entry.

I grunted a reply as I moved across the threshold. I was unsure how exactly to handle this situation. I had expected screaming, possibly even additional name-calling.

"Grams call you?" I asked, my arms folding stiffly in front of me.

"Yeah," he answered, packing a few items into his suitcase before sliding the zipper. Straightening, he looked at me with big brown eyes. I could tell he wanted to talk about it.

"Let's go," I said.

Jerry followed me silently to the SUV.

"Put your bag in the backseat," I ordered him.

"What's wrong with the trunk?" he asked with attitude, my tone clearly bothering him.

"It's full."

"Oh."

Buckling up, I waited until he got his ass in the car, but not for the door to shut before I pulled away from the curb.

He grunted a response, nothing more. Okay, so I was still exceptionally pissed the fuck off about his comments.

"I'm sorry." Jerry tried.

"Don't be, Jerry. Never apologize for speaking the truth."

Chapter 8

"Do you want one room or two?" I asked, shutting off the SUV in front of a clean, well-maintained hotel on the outskirts of Madison, Ohio. It was several steps up from my usual, but lower than when I had traveled with Blake, which I was not thinking about.

"Whatever," he groaned, blinking back sleep, which had been his primary contribution to the mission thus far.

I got one room, for several reasons: one, I'm cheap; two, it would force us to talk and either work this out or drive a solid wedge between us; and three, I didn't want to be alone.

I'll never admit the third.

Jerry showered as I reviewed the photos on my laptop again. If I had thought the giant talking snakes had been strange, this was beyond my descriptive abilities.

Smelling like fresh oranges, Jerry sat down next to me in flannel pajama pants and a white shirt.

"Any guess on what it is?" he asked, sitting close to me.

I sighed, pushing the laptop closer to him. "Yes, and I hope I'm wrong."

"Are we good?" Jerry asked, staring at the laptop and not at me.

I shrugged. It was foolish thinking I could build a life outside of being an Executioner, and his words only reminded me of that.

"Yep. I'm going to shower. Try and get some sleep, the detectives will want us there early tomorrow."

"You mean today?"

I checked my watch with a grunt. "Yeah, today."

He nodded, watching surreptitiously as I walked away from him. I could feel my old walls rebuilding and I was grateful for them. They kept the pain and misery down where it belonged.

...

Dawn found me awake, staring out the one window in our room and listening to Jerry snore.

I missed Blake. I missed having the tender beginnings of a real life. I wanted more than running from state to state eliminating problems. I wanted—I

62

wanted what I couldn't fucking have. Dwelling on it wouldn't do any damn good.

I flipped open the three ring binder, looking for when the continental breakfast opened. I had a few hours until the promised waffles and donuts were available, so I opted for the gym to kill some time. Jerry could get a few more hours of sleep.

I twisted my growing locks back into a loose bun, rolling my shoulders as I took the elevator down. Pushing open the glass door to the gym, I scowled at the guy on the treadmill. He was too busy chatting on his phone to notice me.

I slouched over to the rowing machine, having more aggression to work out.

...

Sweat-drenched and feeling mildly better, I headed back to the room. Hopefully Jerry would be up. If nothing else, I could shower and get breakfast.

I stopped short at the door, hearing his muffled voice. Physically I felt his anguish and sweet relief.

Huffing, I leaned against the wall, waiting, something I've never done well.

Down the hall, a room door opened. Laughter spilled out, along with an adorable blond boy who scampered away from his chasing father's teasing noises. Easily catching him, the equally blond father sprayed kisses against his son's cheeks as the laughing turned to squealing. Closing the door behind them was a heavily pregnant mother, who casually draped an arm around her husband's waist before also kissing her son.

I watched with fucking tears in my eyes, jealous.

Growling, I opened the door, not able to wait any longer.

"Yeah, me too. I'll call you soon," Jerry finished up quickly before looking my way.

I should have asked about Mark, but I didn't, as I slammed myself into the bathroom to shower.

Anger, rage, and self-loathing hit my shields with force. I showered and dressed quickly before emerging from the bathroom.

Jerry was dressed professionally compared to my jeans and black shirt. His dress pants and white button down were immaculately pressed after being stowed for so long.

"Magic iron?" I asked gruffly, breaking the silence between us.

He smiled, and for at least a few moments the young, carefree Jerry I had first met was back. "I'll never tell."

I felt the corner of my lip twitch in a smile in spite of myself.

"So, you want to talk about anything?" he asked as we headed to the free breakfast before leaving.

"Don't eat if you won't be able to handle what is coming next. I'm not cleaning puke off my shoes." I leaned back against the elevator wall.

He looked at me sideways, exiting into the lobby.

"I'm going to throw my bag into the car," I added. He nodded at me before heading to breakfast.

I wasn't attached to the things in the bag, but I didn't want to go shopping again.

Finally presented with the chance to get some much needed fuel, I loaded my plate full of carbs and a few items of fruit.

I sat down next to Jerry, whose own plate was far more respectable with bacon and a bagel.

"Why don't you eat meat, Olie?" he asked out of idle curiosity.

I could brush it off, but I decided a topic change was exactly what my brain needed, less some key details about Selena.

"When I was five I was given a pet puppy. I named her Beth. She slept with me, ran with me, ate what I ate, and I loved her. She was a bright spot in my otherwise pathetic existence."

I drained my orange juice before my next statement. "The people who raised me stopped feeding me until I killed and ate her. I held off for days but survival is a hard instinct to override." At least it was then. If I had known what my future held, I might have just succumbed to starvation.

Jerry swallowed his bacon with a disgusted look before pushing his plate away. "What kind of dog was she?"

I shrugged. "I don't know."

"What happened to the people who raised you?" His disgust was replaced by anger.

"I killed them, all of them." I had been sharing too much of my past with too many. Blake was a mistake I wouldn't make again, on so many levels.

Jerry nodded and I stood, throwing my trash away. "If you are going to throw up, do it here."

64

He shook his head, losing the carefree youth, as the hardened mage took his place. "I'm good."

"How's Mark?" I asked as we exited into the early morning light.

Dammit to hell I felt bad for walking in.

His smile made me glad I had asked. "Good, really good."

I nodded. "You'd make an excellent parent," I offered.

He blew out a breath as we climbed into the SUV. "I don't want to put an innocent life in danger because of who I am and what I've done."

I couldn't help but laugh. "I think you are overreaching on your enemies."

He smiled, but it was strained. "Maybe."

...

We arrived at the cemetery twenty minutes later, and it was a zoo.

"Holy fucking hell," Jerry whispered, covering his nose as we exited the SUV. The stench of death, decay, and rotting bodies assaulted our noses.

I raised an eyebrow at him, trying to judge if he was going to puke. Shaking his head, he pulled it together.

"I'm good," he croaked out.

Turning back to the scene in front of me, I walked toward the yellow crime scene tape and a plainclothes officer in a tweed suit.

"Excuse me, I'm looking for Detective Miller."

He turned dark eyes, sizing me up before returning his gaze to my sea green ones. I had already given him the once over upon approaching.

"Who's asking?"

"Your fairy godmother."

He grunted, "Olivia, Executioner from the Council." Nodding, he held the yellow tape up so Jerry and I could cross under.

"I'm Miller." He turned, looking over the cemetery. His bewilderment was evident.

"Can you take me through it from the beginning?" I asked.

He nodded, about to begin when a large officer bellowed at us.

"Whoa Miller, who the hell do you think you are bringing them in here? This isn't a damn attraction." One of the uniformed guards stopped the gray-haired Miller with a forceful hand to the chest.

"Back off Daniels," Miller growled in response, pushing the hand off and stepping into the giant's personal space. "These are the Supernatural Council's representatives."

I moved forward, extending my hand. "Olivia, Head Executioner." I loved the way his eyes widened. "This is Jerry, Head Transporter."

Jerry quickly shook off his stare of disbelief at me for assigning him a position as he shook Daniels's hand. I wanted to call him Head Mage, but they hadn't exactly come out to the public at large. Granted, from the little news I saw, humans were demanding to know what other species were out there.

We just weren't obliging.

Daniels ran a hand over his shaggy hair. "I apologize. It's been a long night keeping reporters and civilians out of here."

"I can imagine," I said with a nod. I wish I had known they were here last night. Talk about wasting time sleeping.

"The dead just don't disappear," Daniels stated, clearly having a hard time with the situation.

"No," I agreed, "they don't." Even vampires left dust behind.

"I'm going to take them through the time line. Since you were first to arrive, do you want to accompany me?" Miller asked.

Daniels nodded, falling in step with us.

"The caretaker was out here at four in the morning tending to the lawn, removing trash and such when he found this." Miller waved his hand toward the 52 empty graves. I could imagine his brain was having a hard time processing what he saw: these graves had been dug *out of*, not into. As Daniels said, the dead don't disappear.

"After he recovered from the shock, he heard chanting and followed it," Daniels took over seamlessly. "He saw four women holding hands and chanting in dark robes, with a woman in white in the middle."

Jerry's quick inhale had both men turning to him. "Does that mean something?" Daniels asked observantly.

Jerry turned to me and I shook my head. "Let's get all the facts first," I advised.

He nodded mutely.

"Let's see the site of said chanting," I asked. Alright, I attempted to ask. It came out as more of a command.

Both men started to walk as Jerry and I fell behind a step.

"Olie," Jerry hissed, infusing his fear and worry in my name.

"I know," I answered, annoyed.

Next to a towering stone crypt with the name Morrison etched into it was a makeshift altar of blue cloth. Upon it rested incense and a bowl holding something truly rank smelling. Around the circle were the bodies of three dead witches.

"There's so much blood," Jerry whispered, picking his leg up only to feel his shoe pulling free from the gore with a sticky sound. That had him gulping down his breakfast.

Crouching down to the bowl I asked, "Do you have gloves?"

Miller and Daniels both provided me a pair. I handed one back to Jerry, watching as his dark skin turned slightly ashen.

"You good?" I asked.

He nodded, giving me a tight-lipped smile.

I snapped the gloves on and poked around in the bowl, wishing for a shifters sense of smell as I inhaled deeply.

Standing up, I handed the bowl to Jerry, not getting much off it. He repeated what I had done. Moving to the victims, I rolled the first one to her back. Dark brown locks were plastered together with her sticky blood. Her face was frozen in surprise, her throat neatly sliced open. Moving to the others I found much the same, except that in the case of the last, her face was frozen in anger. I could almost hear the scream on her pale lips.

With a groan I stood back up, looking over the graveyard.

"All the bodies are gone." It was a statement, not a question.

"All," Daniels said, paling slightly.

"How did they move all the bodies?" Miller asked, with a mix of awe and fear.

Jerry answered after setting the bowl back down with a grim expression. "Nobody moved the bodies. They walked off."

Pinching the bridge of my nose, I turned to the pale-faced officers, "We need to speak with the caretaker." I removed my gloves, hoping I hadn't smeared dried blood on my face.

"Dead bodies do not get up and walk." Daniels heavily emphasized each word.

I cast a look at Jerry, who shook his head, also removing his gloves. Daniels was in way over his head.

"The caretaker, please," I repeated, about done being nice. His inability to process reality was not my problem.

Miller responded, moving away from Daniels, who just stood there too dumbfounded to move.

Cracking my neck, I scanned the overly bright day. I should have worn a coat; the sun wasn't doing much to dispel the cold here. Miller led us back deeper into the property and under another yellow police tape line, taking a small, worn path that we walked down single file. The path opened up into a flourishing clearing with a full garden in the front yard of the dwelling.

Our knock on the door was greeted with a disgruntled, "Enter."

Miller opened the door and stepped back. "I need to check on Daniels."

I nodded, pushing into the quaint home, not expecting the sight that greeted my eyes.

Intelligent emerald eyes sized me up. He sat puffing on a pipe in front of a low fire, recognition flaring in his gaze.

"Executioner," he greeted me, tipping his head in respect.

"Have we met before?"

The orange haired leprechaun shook his head, pulling his blanket firmly around his shoulder. "Nay—though you did end my third cousin once removed. I'm Fergus, Fergus McLawson."

His look of contempt had me crossing my arms. "I'm sure he deserved it."

The leprechaun spat in the fire. "Aye, that he did."

Turning his wrinkled face back to us, he asked, "What do ye want?"

Jerry stepped forward. "We are trying to figure out what happened."

"Bah," Fergus spat, "ain't it obvious?"

"It would be, except witches and necromancers don't work together," I answered.

Satisfaction lit Fergus's eyes. "You know what the woman in white is?"

"I do," I answered.

He nodded. "Perhaps rumors of your incompetence have been exaggerated."

I huffed.

"Ye will be interested to know she was bound with enchanted silver cuffs."

"Fucking hell," I hissed, rubbing my eyes.

"How powerful were the witches—any mages?" Jerry questioned, maintaining his composure.

"Nay, hardly a blip on my radar. I thought the wee ones were playing out there again, until the white woman tapped her power. Bloody hell, I almost lost my supper."

Jerry sighed and looked at me, silently asking if I had any more questions. I didn't.

"Don't run off, Fergus," I warned him as we left.

"You sound like the bloody bobby!" he called after us.

"Where do you think they learned their best moves from?" I yelled back, not bothering to turn.

A scuffling sound had me turning to see his hunched figure at the door, his eyes serious. "Be careful Executioner, the witches are up to something revolting."

I sighed, "Any idea what it is?"

He nodded. "Trust me, ye do not want to know."

I smiled, showing my teeth. "Do not presume to speak my mind for me, Fergus."

Shifting, he lowered his eyes, "The rumor is the witches are trying to open a portal to the Fae."

He was right, I didn't want to know. I couldn't hide the look of pure terror or the blood leaving my face.

Fergus nodded. "Glad to see ye have a healthy respect for that power."

With that, he slammed the door on us.

It took a few moments before I could focus on Jerry in front of me. Grasping my shoulder, he shook me slightly.

"Olivia, the witches can't contact the Fae."

I gulped. "I fucking hope not, or we are all doomed."

...

Jerry walked around the graves, taking time to stare down into the holes with a mixture of intensity and horror. Some unknown witch had a small fucking army of zombies, not to mention a necromancer, at her disposal.

Fuck.

My ass started playing, "Move Bitch (Get Out the Way)."

"Dammit, Tommy," I hissed, pulling out my phone. Then I chimed, "Speak of the devil! Tommy, what are you doing?" I couldn't help the smile in my voice.

"OLIE!" he shouted. "Disneyland is amazing. I miss you!"

"I miss you too, bud."

"You've gotta come out here, Olie, the rides are awesome. The parades are out of this world! Not to mention all the different worlds, we haven't even been to half of them yet."

"That's wonderful."

"Okay, I gotta go. Love you, Olie!"

The phone clicked off before I could respond.

"Kids?" Miller asked, coming to stand next to me.

"Yeah," I answered, not elaborating. I refocused on the case as Jerry came to stand before me with a distant look in his dark eyes.

"Anything?" I asked.

He shook his head. "Nothing we didn't already know."

I nodded, stowing my phone again.

"What's our next move?" Miller asked.

"For you, nothing," I sighed. "For us, there are avenues we can attempt."

Miller shifted, uncomfortable with my honesty. "Don't take offense, Miller. I'll update you on what we find out and worst case, if these things kill us, the Council will have your information.

He regarded me closely, his eyes searching my own. "You go after dangerous shit a lot?

"Yep."

"Death wish?"

"Killing keeps me sane," I admitted.

He shook his head, moving away.

"Any spells you can cast to lead us to the mysterious witch?" I asked Jerry.

He chewed his lip thoughtfully. "Maybe, if we can find a local shop."

I nodded, heading to the SUV.

Daniels ambushed us, grabbing my arm and spinning me forcefully around to face him.

"Where do you think you are going?" he demanded.

Slowly, my eyes trailed up from his hand resting on my bare skin to his eyes.

"Uhh, you need to be letting her go now." Jerry reached over to remove his hand.

"Don't," I hissed.

Daniels shifted his focus from Jerry back to me, "You need to explain—"

Rage swelled and I hit him full force with fear—weak-in-the-knees, pee-yourself, can't-breathe fear. His reaction was exactly as advertised, dropping to his knees, trembling. I lifted his hand off my arm and bent down to his ear. "No one touches me."

With that, I walked away. "When the fuck did witches start binding necromancers?" I asked Jerry.

He gave me a wide berth after my power display.

"I don't know Olie, but was that necessary?"

I turned on him quickly, stepping into his personal space. I'll give him props for not backing up at the intensity in my eyes. "The moment I allow the humans' government to dictate what I do is the moment we are all lost. These interactions are far more important than one human's hurt ego. My power keeps us all safe. Do not forget get that."

Jerry lowered his head slightly before following me to the SUV.

I should stop trying to keep friends. I wasn't built for it.

...

"Turn right in five hundred feet," the GPS's curt voice informed me.

"What's it called again?" I asked.

Jerry checked his phone. "The Bitchy Witchy."

"I'll fit right in."

Jerry snorted, "That you will."

Dammit, me and my trying.

The small parking lot was deserted and we didn't have a long walk to the blacked out glass door entrance.

The overpowering reek of smoke blasted out of the shop. My eyes were having a hard time adjusting from the bright sunny day to the dark, cluttered interior.

"I ain't buying nothin'!" yelled a rattling voice.

Jerry pushed in front of me to greet the hunched over witch hobbling toward us, leaning heavily on her cane.

"I'd like to purchase."

She squinted up at him with a huff before turning to me. "You wait here."

I nodded, annoyed. Why did I always have to stay out in the lobby when the witches were talking? Fucking Blake had me do the same thing.

My jaw tightened, my eyes misting of their own damn accord. Fucking hell, I had to give up. I had to move on. My fucking heart wasn't letting me. I just missed the asshole so much.

After ten minutes I went back to the car to wait for Jerry. Unlike in the other shop, I was fairly certain I was not allowed to peruse the wares.

...

Grams called just as Jerry was climbing into the SUV, probably missing driving his Beast around.

"Olivia." Her tone had warning signals spiking through my veins.

"What?" I clipped out.

"Do not break anything."

"Maybe I should drive," Jerry offered.

Tapping the steering wheel, I nodded my head in agreement and we made the switch.

"Alright, go ahead."

"We've been invited to Blake and Angelina's wedding."

Rage colored my vision, a snarl leaving my lips without my permission. "No."

Grams cleared her throat, "No!" I reaffirmed.

Softly, so as not to disturb my already delicate sanity: "We are head of the Supernatural Council, dear."

I sat back against the seat with an audible thump, causing Jerry to flinch from the sudden movement.

"No," I tried again with less hope.

"Just think about it," Grams concluded with a sigh.

Think about it? Think about the only man I'd ever allowed myself to love marrying someone else?

"Nothing good can come of this," I muttered, rubbing my forehead. "When is it?" Maybe I could just conveniently forget. Yeah, no one was going to buy that excuse.

"Two weeks."

"WHAT?" Jerry and I asked in unison.

"Two weeks," Grams repeated.

I groaned, "I hope I get taken by the witches."

"Olivia," Grams scolded, "do not even think of allowing that to happen in order to get out of going."

I groaned again.

Noise from the children colored the line. "Think about it," Grams repeated before ending the call.

"He still loves you," Jerry stated confidently.

"Ha," I humorlessly replied. "Why then, wise man, is he marrying another woman?"

Jerry was silent, so I answered for him. "Because she can solve his problems. I can't, because I will always and forever be a demon whore." I hissed the last two words.

Jerry shifted in the driver's seat, clearly having no idea how to answer that.

"I don't know about that, but I do know Angelina feels threatened by you. That's why she invited you."

"She invited me because I am the Head Executioner for the Council."

"Really?" he asked, looking at me for a brief moment as we made a right turn. "How many weddings do you get invited to yearly?"

He had a point. It wasn't one I was willing to concede, though. "There's our hotel."

He grunted, my blaringly obvious topic change noted.

...

"This is taking forever," I complained again, watching Jerry sitting cross-legged on the navy carpet of the hotel room, with bowls, ingredients, and books spread around him.

Perched on the bed, I rested my chin in my hand, lying on my stomach.

"It's an art form," he replied through clenched teeth.

I huffed, rolling to my back to stare at the ceiling.

As is a common theme in my life, I didn't wait well.

Jerry grunted and I rolled back over to his look of satisfaction.

"Done."

"Where is she?"

He sighed. "It didn't exactly work out like that."

"Why not?"

"She shielded at the graveyard. I was able to create a locator so that in a 100 yard radius, or so, you can track her, like playing a game of hot and cold."

I pursed my lips at him. I wasn't celebrating this as a win.

"If you knew anything about magic you would be applauding my immense talent and skills right now."

I slow clapped, "Woohoo."

"Rude."

"If you want recognition, hang out with your own kind."

He huffed, "No thank you. I like my head on my shoulders, and those bitches are not fans of all this awesomeness. And now, I'm going to shower.

"Here," he handed me the gold talisman. "Hot and cold."

Right now it was cold, very cold. Where the hell did an army of zombies wander off to?

...

Jerry exited the shower a few minutes later. "How long can the necromancer keep the zombies above ground?" I asked.

"No idea. I've only encountered their kind twice, and neither was a pleasant experience."

I grunted, "Same here. They are fucking creepy."

"Agreed."

After a pause, he asked, "Did you notice the footprints at the graveyard?"

"Nope."

Jerry chewed his bottom lip. "Me either."

"Portal?"

Jerry sat heavily. "The blood sacrifice would make more sense. It wasn't for the necromancer. She would have been fully charged in the cemetery."

"Anyway to track a portal?"

"No, and the talisman is worthless until they come back."

I nodded, "They will."

"Unless they made it to the Fae."

I blew out a breath, stowing the gold in my jeans pocket. "If the only thing that happened from the witches reaching the Fae was their disappearance, I'd go to the fucking wedding with bells on."

"Have you decided if you are going?"

"Do I have a choice?"

"No, I suppose you don't."

We scoured the entire state in the week and a half before I had to be back for the wedding, and even though I spent a small fortune on gas, there was nothing to be found.

Chapter 9

If I was hoping for a happy ending with Blake, that he would leave Angelina and run into my arms with a heartfelt apology and an earnest declaration of his love, I was fucking deluding myself.

"Olivia, are you ready?" Grams called out, coming down the stairs into the living room.

"Yeah," I grumbled back.

Tommy looked up at me as I gave him back the controller to the racing game he was destroying me in. He might have been a teenager, but by the sorrowful expression in his eyes and the soft squeeze of my hand, he understood.

Grams raked over my outfit, finding it fitting. The short purple dress ended mid-thigh, embellished with large rhinestones on the strapless top. It matched the purple highlights in my hair, which was pulled into a soft bun behind my left ear.

"Are you bringing any weapons?"

I sighed, following her to the garage. "No, you've made it perfectly clear we are to be an open target."

"It's a peaceful event."

"Nothing with the Supernatural community is ever peaceful, but at least Darren and Logan will be there. They grow claws." I was still fucking jealous.

"Mercer will be there running security."

"Really, humans doing security?"

"The Centennial House is using Darren's firm for security."

I cast her a sidelong look as we got into my SUV. I could at least have my toys waiting for me, even if she was driving. "When did Mercer make that switch?"

"Soon after he lost his job," she answered sadly. "Terrible shame about that."

I nodded, unsure who should be ashamed. "Have you talked to Hash about it?"

"I have. He can't overlook the conflict of interest."

"Ugh, like Franks is a model officer. What ever happened with the case?"

"We won. They settled out of court once they saw the pictures of the untreated wounds on your back."

"Good, that makes me feel slightly better about not killing him. I'd absolutely still do it if I happened upon him in a dark alley."

Grams laughed, "Or a well-lit alley."

"I'm not particular."

...

An hour later we pulled up to The Eagle, an elite and highly restrictive club I had only heard mentions of before.

I grudgingly had to admit it was elegant and awe-inspiring.

The valet took my keys and I watched them wistfully as my trunk full of weapons was carted away.

"Come, let's see Darren and Kass," Grams said, pulling me behind her gracefully. I straightened my shoulders, pretending I wasn't the grieving, miserable, ex-girlfriend, but the confident Executioner.

Kass took one look at me and pulled me into an embrace. "How ya doing?" she asked kindly, her dark eyes sincere.

"Fucking wonderful."

She grimaced. "So, we found out the sex."

"Really?" I perked up at that news, eyeing her hand resting lovingly on her stomach.

"It's a boy."

"Aww! Congrats!"

Kass beamed, "Thanks, he's totally healthy, nothing to worry about."

I smiled, squeezing her hand. "That's wonderful news."

Mercer stopped by, dropping a kiss on Grams's cheek as he checked in. He looked better in this environment. The suit and the technology peeking out his ear were both of a far higher quality. I daresay he even looked more relaxed, but that could have just been all the sex he was having with Grams.

Jerry and Mark found us next, looking better together, though their body language still hinted at trouble. Mark, also dressed for security, gave Jerry a pointed look that reaffirmed my suspicions before moving away. Although neither Mercer nor Mark moved far from our little group, I suppose I wasn't the only one not really thrilled about the no weapons policy.

Logan and Lorraine found us next, hooray.

Lorraine, as per usual, was drunk. How did the bitch find the alcohol so fast? If I didn't find her annoying and idiotic I'd be tagging along for the drinks. As it was, however, I wanted to throttle her.

Logan looked at me over her head, which was leaning unsteadily against him.

"How are you?" he asked, sincerely, which for the record freaked me out.

I shrugged, not trusting my voice, my misty eyes looking away from his quickly.

"Let's get you a drink," Kass suggested, pulling me gently behind her.

I nodded, grateful for the escape.

Blowing out a trapped breath, I gave the bartender a closed lip smile as I plunked down with a thump at the bar.

"Wine?" the bartender asked.

I nodded. He poured a glass quickly, not bothering to ask what kind. Good, I wasn't particular.

"Sorry Kass, I know you can't drink right now."

She shrugged, toying with the napkin under her ginger ale. "Not a big deal, Olie."

Right, the big deal was that I was here.

A throat cleared behind me. Turning, I looked into intelligent green eyes I hadn't seen in quite some time. "Morgan," I acknowledged, nodding at his blond date as well.

"Olivia, it's been too long. Any succubus you need us to drain?" His meaning was not lost on me.

I grunted a reply, turning back to my drink. Asking that Master, Vampire, asshole for help with a first blood rage incubus was clearly not one of my better moments of judgment. Like Tate, he controlled a large House in St Ann. I had reached out for assistance when an incubus had accidentally drawn first blood at Kitten.

He left his date and slid next to my free side, his designer suit pressing against my forearm resting on the bar. Gently, he trailed his perfectly manicured fingers over my wrist.

"I've heard rumors of your..." He paused, looking for the correct word, finally deciding on, "...bedroom savvy," his eyes aglow with the trademark amber of a vampire either aroused or pissed off. I was betting on the first.

I raised an eyebrow. Blake was fucking telling stories of our lovemaking?

"Perhaps you would be so kind as to give a few lessons."

I groaned. This was such a mistake coming here.

"Fuck off, Morgan."

His gentle caress turned into a painful grab. Behind me I heard Kass yell for Darren. I didn't need help, I was a fucking succubus able to control and manipulate emotions. Granted, I couldn't push unwanted emotions, but I sure could help what was already there.

"Careful. I have the advantage here." Morgan hissed.

I thought about pumping him full of fear, but that didn't feel right. Anger, though, now that I could use. I let the heated emotions swarm our contact. Blind, furious anger, a fury of hatred ran through my veins, merging with Morgan's skin.

Fear flashed once in those brilliant green depths and he tried to break the contact. I didn't let him, clamping my hand over his. I wasn't fucking done. Let the asshole try to contain all of this anger and not get himself into trouble.

"Olivia," Darren said softly behind me.

"Don't touch her," Kass warned.

"Olivia," he tried again.

A warm hand rested on my bare shoulder, squeezing gently before the voice commanded, "Release him."

I did. Morgan nodded to Logan before rubbing his wrist, then plastering on a fake smile as he went back to his date.

I didn't turn to either of them. "He deserved it. You should have heeded Kass's warning, Logan. What I was pushing into him would affect you as well."

Logan shrugged, apparently unaffected, or at least doing a better job of controlling it than Morgan.

"They are all going to be after you tonight," Darren informed me, his eyes sweeping the area for threats.

"Because I'm such a great fuck?" I drained my wine, waving the empty glass at the bartender for more.

Darren moved into my personal space, and he was fucking lucky he was married to my friend. "This is not a wise decision," I informed him, whispering softly so others wouldn't overhear us.

Logan gave a short chuckle. "You are going to want to hear this, actually.

"Blake is claiming you ruined him for other women. That's why he hasn't been able to perform his usual duties leading up to the wedding."

I'm pretty sure my mouth hung open in shock.

Logan leaned in, whispering against my ear, "It's also a matter of speculation whether he will be able to close the deal tonight."

"That's insane," I hissed back. "I've slept with lots and lots of humans as well as Supernaturals, and no one has ever claimed I ruined them."

Logan shrugged, a coy smile playing on his lips. "He also gave that as the reason he accosted you in the tech lab."

I groaned, resting my head against the bar. "Please tell me there is no video of that."

Darren patted my back gently. "You looked great in it."

"Darren," Kass whispered with reprimand, looking around us.

Fucking Jerry was right on the money with his assessment of why I was invited.

"There is even a bet if Angelina will invite you into the marriage bed tonight. As you know, the blood exchange and sex seal the deal between the two Houses."

I groaned, "I'm aware. Let's just hope my influence has worn off."

Kass cleared her throat before leaning forward. "How long ago was the video?"

I chewed on my thumb thoughtfully. "When was I chaperoning Darren?"

A look of confusion crossed Kass's face. "You slept with him that same day?"

I nodded, draining my wine glass again, opting for beer this time—well, if this fancy ass establishment had any.

"Why didn't you say anything?"

"What was there to say? Yes, I slept with Blake. No, he doesn't want me back, claimed it was a mistake. That's nothing I care to repeat."

"Your emotional ties should be cut at least, that was about a month ago," Kass reminded me.

"I almost wish he could feel me now." I hushed myself, sealing my emotions behind solid walls, pushing my shoulders back.

Clearing my throat, I turned in my seat, which I was certain was real leather, as Grams and Jerry made their way over. I lifted my beer in a toast before draining half of it.

...

"I can't believe I'm actually here," I muttered to myself, leaning against a thick white Roman column, hiding. I'm not proud of it, but being at Blake's wedding, alone, sucked. I struggled through the ceremony, the shitty comments and sly looks, but now, as the last dance was slowly approaching, I was ready to leave.

I blew out a breath and ruffled my newly cut bangs, which settled at an angle just below my eyebrow. The soft curls framed my face, but even that wasn't enough to get Blake back, nothing was.

"How's it going Olie?" Kass asked, slipping next to me.

I groaned, holding out my empty champagne glass.

"Yeah, about the same here," she confided. "At least you can drink."

"True," I agreed, my eyes locked onto the happy bride and groom.

Blake was devastating in his tux, easily leading his bride and mate around the dance floor. I tried to crush the sorrow swelling inside of me, but it didn't work. The best I could hope for was that it didn't seep past my barriers. It wouldn't, but a small part of me wished it would. It had been weeks since I slept with him and I knew he couldn't feel me anymore, but I wanted him to. I wanted him to know the depth of my pain and devastation.

Lorraine drunkenly staggered next to us and I closed my eyes, willing myself not to kill her.

"So," she slurred, already testing my patience, "do you ever wonder what is so wrong with you that no one wants to marry you?"

Logan and Darren appeared then. Logan pulled Lorraine behind him. I just smiled, my eyes riveted to Blake.

"No Lorraine, I don't wonder. I know what's wrong with me." Demon whore, that's all I would ever be.

"Aren't you supposed to be planning my wedding?" Lorraine drawled, coming out from behind Logan.

The bitch had a point.

...

81

The bride and groom were sent off and I hid in the shadows, not that it was really hiding. With vampires' sight, they could all see me.

Kass wrapped her shawl around her shoulders with a heavy sigh, leaning against me. "I have to go pick up a forgotten ear piece in the groom's room, then we can head out."

"I'll get it. Go with Grams and get off your feet."

She smiled. "Thanks."

I nodded, turning back to the huge expanse of wedding venue.

After three wrong turns and finally being escorted by the caterer, I found the groom's room. Without thought, I opened the door, casting a look around at the discarded clothing, hangers, and tux bags.

"If I were an ear piece, where would I be?" I muttered, looking around.

"What did you—" Blake's voice died as he came around the corner. I backed up, terrified.

"What the fuck are you doing in here?" I all but screamed at him.

"Shh," he coaxed, closing the distance between us.

"Don't fucking shush me." I was furious at him. Furious he left me, furious he seduced me, blamed me, and taped me. All the fury was covering up a swell of pain I was having a hard time keeping within my shields.

"You told everyone I—" My angry outburst was stopped cold when his lips caressed mine.

"I've missed you," he whispered against my overheated ear, "and your blood."

"No," I whimpered, pushing away from him. The blood of succubi held power for vampires, a natural aphrodisiac that he apparently thought he would need to seal the deal with Angelina.

He didn't let me get far, wrapping his arms around my hips from behind me. Instinct had me tipping my head up as he sank his fangs into my neck.

I exhaled in a heated rush. "No," I whispered again, trying to break free. Damn my traitorous body, damn him for knowing exactly how to seduce me.

"Let me go, please," I begged, unable to move myself.

"Let her go," growled Logan, standing outlined in the doorframe, hands fisted at his sides.

Blake released me and I ran into Logan's arms, trembling. Not my finest moment.

"That's all I was after, bro. Have fun with her."

I heard the door close behind him. I couldn't look Logan in the eyes.

He pulled away and I took the hint, pulling back to wrap my arms around myself, pretending I wasn't so fucking weak-willed that I would have given in to Blake again in the feeble hope he'd take me back on his wedding day. What the fuck is wrong with me?

"Nothing," Logan answered, tilting my chin up, looking at the bite mark on my neck.

"I didn't mean to say that aloud. He didn't heal the bite, did he?"

Logan shook his head, his caramel eyes darkening with his lion. It was the ultimate disrespect.

I squeezed my eyes closed against the wash of self-hatred and hot tears threatening to thread down my cheeks.

With a hiss I dug my fingernails into my palms.

"Enough, Olie." Logan's voice was soft as he pulled me into his arms.

"I don't want your pity," I grumbled at him, my voice muffled by his crisp shirt.

"Will you take my compassion?"

I grunted a noncommittal reply.

Once I had control again, I pulled back, looking into those raw sienna depths. "I came in here looking for a missing earbud."

Logan smiled, turning me toward the exit. "And I came in here to tell you I have it."

"I'm glad you showed up," I sighed. "But I won't admit that to anyone."

He chuckled, slipping an arm around my shoulder. "Wouldn't dream of it."

Chapter 10

It was a week later. A boring week later and I couldn't help but feel this was the calm before the storm. The zombies still hadn't made an appearance, and it was worrying both Jerry and me.

Grams had reached out to the necromancer community, but they didn't want our help locating their missing member. Assholes.

So here I was sitting at Kass's, watching some kids' TV program and playing with Hannah.

"Logan is coming over for dinner tonight," Kass informed me, turning off the TV.

"Is that a hint I need to get gone?" I asked, dressing a doll in an evening gown for Hannah.

"No, it's more of a warning. What's going on between you two?"

I groaned, "Shit if I know."

"The blind hatred seems to be dulling, at least on his end."

"I never hated him. I hate his choice in life partners."

Kass laughed, "Don't we all."

"She's a hussy," Hannah added.

"Agreed," I laughed.

"I heard things were hot and heavy with your last undercover assignment in the strip club," Darren hinted, coming in from the garage and picking up a squealing Hannah. Damn shifter hearing.

I shrugged. The kiss had been intense, complete with roaming hands and a raging hard-on. "I'd like to put that in a pile of things I don't plan on talking about."

Darren laughed. "Like how we don't talk about your ability to do magic?"

"Exactly, I don't do magic and Logan and I hate each other. End of story."

Darren laughed, kissing Kass before heading down the hallway.

Kass raised an eyebrow at me as I went to start washing lettuce.

"Not dealing with it."

"I heard you the first time."

...

The doorbell announced Logan's arrival.

84

Kass and I were setting the table when a freshly washed Hannah screeched down the hall, "I'LL GET IT!"

Darren followed her out, his dress shirt sleeves rolled up as he watched his daughter let his brother in.

"Did you bring the hussy?" Hannah asked, all business.

"I did not," replied Logan.

Hannah moved aside. "You may enter."

I laughed, "Nice work, kid."

Hannah high fived me before wrapping herself around Kass' legs.

"You teach her that?" Logan asked, sitting down heavily.

"Nope, you can't teach good taste."

He grunted a reply.

"Grams get in touch with you about arbitration tomorrow?"

I groaned, sitting next to him. "I'll be there with bells on."

"I wanna wear bells!" Hannah screeched, jumping up and down in her seat.

"Did you feed her sugar?" Kass accused me.

"Sugar, what is this substance you speak of?"

"Yeah she did!" Hannah ratted on me.

"You are cut off," I informed her.

...

Dishes were done, leftovers stashed, and a finally-sleepy Hannah tucked into bed as Logan and I walked outside.

I inhaled the crisp night air, feeling the cool breeze against my skin.

Logan stopped next to my driver's door. "What?" I asked, looking around for trouble.

He sighed, running a hand through his lengthening locks. "You're vulnerable."

"Fuck you."

He shook his head with an easy smile. "Your emotional state."

"I'm unbalanced."

He actually laughed at that, it looked good on him. "Right, but the other shifters tomorrow are going to sense the change in you. They are going to want to help."

I kept glaring at him as he moved into my personal space. "And shifters comfort by touching," he informed me, running his hands under my jacket. Through the thin material of my shirt I could feel his heat.

It should have put me on guard. Instead I ducked my head under his chin, relaxing my shoulders.

"I don't like being touched by strangers."

"But this you are going to accede to?"

"Don't sound so shocked, even the Executioner needs to feel loved," I whispered.

"I was pretty sure I was going to get hit for this."

"Do you want me to hit you?"

Logan pulled away. "Do you want to hit me?" he asked softly, his face very close to my own.

I socked him in the gut, succeeding in hurting my hand. "Ow, you saw that one coming?"

"I did. Get some rest," he called over his shoulder, removing his warmth. "It's a long ass docket."

"Wonderful," I grumbled.

Chapter 11

The fucker wasn't kidding.

It was a damn zoo out there. Note to self: do not say that out loud. I pushed back the curtain I was hiding behind, turning to Grams. As per usual the shifters met town hall style, and this time I was actually backstage since my invite hadn't been lost by Lorraine. The venue was similar but this was larger, at least twice the size.

Reading my shock, she shrugged.

Logan came from behind her, all business in his camel suit, raising an eyebrow at me.

"After you, oh master," I motioned, smirking.

He cracked a half smile, pushing me out in front of him.

The crowd was instantly silenced. We pulled out our chairs behind a simple wood desk and it was unnaturally loud.

I looked around at all the faces, preparing myself for a very long day, trying to remember to smile and not scowl.

Alec leaned against the podium, casting his trademark devilish grin at the crowd.

"Are we ready to begin?" he asked.

Suddenly, the lights flashed off, plunging us all into darkness. A new light flickered brightly into my eyes.

"What the hell?" I muttered, blocking my eyes with a hand.

"*Find what you were looking for?*" I heard from the speakers in a voice I recognized.

"Turn it off!" Logan bellowed, standing forcefully, sending his chair tumbling backwards.

I stood stiffly, shame turning my face red. Walking to the edge of the stage, I watched Blake stalk me across the Centennial's computer lab.

"*No,*" my small voice on the projection stated.

The grainy footage zoomed in to us kissing, to me pulling back and whispering, "*Blake.*"

From there things got X-rated pretty quickly, but I didn't pull my gaze away.

Logan was still screaming and the tech guys were hustling to cut the feed.

I watched it all, comparing it to my memories. I was a succubus and a woman. What had happened between Blake and me was normal. The unintentional video now being distributed cut a clear path into my prior life. I pulled the strength I needed from those memories. I had survived worse at the hands of Selena. I'd survive this intense invasion of privacy.

Finally it ended. The remarks were not far behind it.

"I wonder how much for a ride."

"Did you see how flexible her hips are?"

"Her shit must be loose."

"I bet I have a chance."

"Whore."

"Demon whore."

"Why does she have a say over us? She's not mated to the Alpha."

I was still staring at the now dark screen. Logan caught my eye as I came back on stage. The lights blinded me yet again as they returned to normal. I closed my eyes, knowing what I'd have to do.

Weakness was not a trait that could go unpunished in our world. I had done an exceptional job hiding my weakness and flaunting my killing, but that fucking video blasted it all to hell. I was vulnerable, weak, and easily manipulated.

That was not the image these shifters would leave with.

"First challenger, let's go!" I bellowed, turning back to the crowd. Several females got up at once, jostling to get to me.

"Form a line, clear the stage!" I ordered, pulling off my jacket and checking my dagger.

Logan moved forward, catching my eye. What he couldn't say was that I didn't have to do this. He could stop it all, sure. But if I allowed him to do that, I might as well release my title and place by his side.

My ego wasn't about to let that happen.

These bitches wanted to see if they were better than me?

Bring it the fuck on.

He saw the determination, the ruthless killer I was known for, and moved to the side to monitor the fights. Suddenly, the large crowds made perfect sense.

What I didn't realize, and wouldn't for some time, was how Logan had known the first line of my unintentional sex tape.

"This is not to the death," Logan commanded. "Subdue only."

Releasing the dagger and holder, I slid it across the stage to rest at his feet. Hand-to-hand it was.

...

I had the eighth or ninth challenger pinned with an arm bar, applying a dangerous amount of pressure to break her arm, and she still wasn't tapping.

"Tap," I commanded.

Still she struggled. "Fine," I grunted, applying the pressure to snap her bones with a dry crack.

She cried out and I held the break apart.

She gasped, her blond hair pooling under her. "You bitch," she panted.

"That's Queen Bitch to you," I hissed, applying more pressure.

"I tap!" She screamed.

I released her, rolling quickly to my feet. The strain of these fights was wearing on me. My shoulders hurt, the right side of my face was swollen, and I was fairly certain I had knocked something important lose in my right knee.

We had been at it for two hours and I needed a break. I wasn't taking one. I was going to finish that damn line.

I almost let my shoulders sag in relief when I saw my line was down to just one young and inexperienced shifter. I had either gone through the line faster than I realized or people were changing their minds. Either way, I was thrilled.

She approached the stage warily.

"Not too late to sit back down," I tried.

Silently she shook her head, her eyes cataloging my injuries. Her left foot tried to land a heavy and slow kick to my right knee. Even in my exhausted state I was faster. Shifting to the left, I reached behind her head, locking her neck into a chokehold.

She bucked and flung, trying to get me off. Keeping my weight low, I tightened my grip.

"Hey Logan, any chance we can order lunch?"

She grunted, pawing at my arm.

"Do not shift," Logan warned before returning his attention to me. "What do you want?"

"Chocolate pie," I groaned, applying still more pressure.

"That's dessert."

"Fine, salad, pasta, breadsticks, and pizza then," I amended my order, releasing the unconscious girl.

After gingerly rolling her to her side, I stood up, brushing my hands on my thighs. "I'm not sharing, either."

Logan huffed and I could see the pride in his eyes. It did strange things to my insides.

"I suppose we still have to arbitrate?" I asked, wanting to sit down but refusing to show weakness or to favor my knee.

"We do," he agreed.

"Delivery?"

"Consider it done."

"I think I'm good for the next month on gym time."

"Not so fast," Lorraine announced, stepping up the stairs. "I challenge you."

I looked to Logan, confused. "Why would you challenge her?" he asked.

"She is acting mate and as your mate I demand a seat next to you. Since you won't give me one, I will just have to take it."

"Can I kill her?" I asked Logan.

"No," he answered quickly.

"Fine, I'll accept kicking her ass."

Stomping across the stage, she moved fast. I bounced on my toes, my body worn.

The little bitch had planned well.

"You can't wait a few months to sit in my spot?" I asked.

She lunged, connecting solidly with my shoulder.

"Ouch," I muttered, massaging the sore muscles. That was about the same force as the shifter hit with.

I wasn't prepared for her speed. Quick punches landed to my midsection, doubling me over and denying my attempt at breathing.

She smiled smugly and I saw it: the raw need, the high in her eyes enhancing her limited human abilities.

"Fuck," I hissed. "Who did you drink from?" I demanded, standing back up.

Fear and uncertainly flashed in her eyes before she spared a moment to look at Logan and back to me. Decision made, she came at me with everything she had, and while it wasn't much, it took more effort than I wanted to expend to take her down to the ground.

Leaning heavily against her ribs I asked again, "Who?"

I heard Logan coming to squat next to me. "Acting mate asked you a question," he growled.

"Screw you both!" she screamed at us. "I don't have to talk to either of you."

"Release her," Logan commanded, touching my arm gently.

I did as he instructed, watching her leave with pure disgust on my face.

"This was planned."

"Yes, but you have proven yourself well," Logan complimented me.

I nodded, turning as the desk and chairs were brought forward. Logan sat down first and I had to ease myself down, trying not to appear too needy for the support of the chair.

...

We made it through the cases before we even finished our meals. Apparently, beating several shifters back to back made everyone far more agreeable to my suggestions.

If it didn't take such a toll, I'd make a habit of it.

"Someone leaked the footage of me and Blake," I whispered softly as we walked to our vehicles.

"Yes," Logan agreed.

"Do you think Lorraine knew it would play here, or was she just thinking quickly on her feet?"

"I don't like your accusations."

I wheeled on him, anger flaring inside. "I don't like being set up."

"I didn't know."

"I'm not sure I believe you."

He shifted his feet before nodding. "I suppose that's fair."

"And the vampire blood she drank?"

He shifted again, settling his hands into his pockets, legs braced wide. "I know where she sleeps."

"Har, har, you're a riot."

...

I settled back against the SUV's seat with a groan. Lorraine had nailed my ribs exceptionally well.

Grams's classical melody chimed on my phone. Starting the SUV, I hit ANSWER.

"What?" I groaned.

"I heard."

I huffed. What was there to say?

"Do you want me to find out who leaked the footage?"

"No, I already have a good guess as to who did that."

Grams voice softened, "Is there anything we can do?"

"No, this isn't even considered betrayal or an act of violence. It's just disgusting and an attempt to make me feel ashamed for having sex."

"You are a good person Olivia."

"I am a succubus and a killer."

Grams sighed, irritated with me. "The zombies have shown up."

"What? Where?"

"The same place you left them."

I groaned, not looking forward to seeing those detectives again.

"Jerry?"

"Awaiting pickup."

...

Grams had a slight hitch in her information. Jerry and Mark were both waiting for me.

I stopped at the curb, rolling down the passenger window.

"I'm looking for a few good zombie killers."

Mark cracked a smile, loading his duffel bag in back before also stowing Jerry's suitcase.

Disgruntled, Jerry motioned me out of the driver's seat. I moved to the back seat, watching the exchange with interest.

Mark took shotgun, sending a warm smile back at me. "How are you holding up?"

I shrugged, not really wanting to dwell on the fact anyone could access a very intimate moment of mine with a click of a button. There were too many memories tied to that particular vulnerability and shame. A very small part of me wondered what Blake felt about it all. His actions in the dressing room were callous and painful. Maybe he had leaked the footage? Maybe he had fed Lorraine his blood?

There was no sense in speculation. Logan said he'd find out. I trusted him to do so.

"So, what about you two?" I asked, looking desperately for a topic change.

"We were denied our application to adopt," Jerry hissed, smashing the gas more than necessary as we sped away from the curb.

Mark smiled, patting Jerry's leg.

"Why?"

"Because I'm a shifter and Jerry is a man."

"What does Jerry being a man have to do with it?"

"The agency won't adopt kids out to same sex parents," Jerry seethed.

Mark's face fell slightly. "But at least we finally made a decision."

Jerry threaded his fingers through Mark's, still on his thigh.

"Anyone else having flashbacks from the first time we met?" I grinned.

Mark laughed. "Did you have any idea saving Hannah would bring about our relationship?"

"Obviously, I did have my crystal ball."

Even Jerry cracked a smile at that.

...

Jerry made excellent time heading back to Ohio. Have I mentioned I detest this state? The streets were filled with snow, unplowed and slick. Jerry gripped the wheel, pulling off the interstate into town.

Mark gave a low whistle as the streetlights illuminated abandoned cars in the middle of the road at awkward angles. A few had run straight into each other; smoke still billowed from the forgotten mess.

A breeze stirred papers. Shops had their pristine windows broken in and snow was slipping into the buildings.

"I really didn't think they would come back here," I whispered, unhappy with myself for not even considering it.

My only consolation was the lack of dead bodies.

"Does a zombie bite turn like a shifter bite?" Mark asked, scanning the area we were crawling through.

"No, but if the zombies do kill a person, the necromancer can reanimate the body," I answered him.

"Ever seen anything like this?" Jerry asked softly, as though scared to break the spell we had wandered into.

"Never," I answered.

"It's like walking into a horror movie," Mark commented as we drove by a pay phone dangling in the soft breeze.

I reached for the file in my bag and pulled out my phone, dialing Detective Miller.

"You really think that's going to work?" Jerry asked, seeing me in the rear view mirror.

"I'm fresh out of ideas."

Jerry nodded before ringing stole my attention.

I sucked in a breath, holding my phone delicately as though one false step on my part would end the call forever.

"Miller," he barked into the speaker.

"It's Olivia, from the Supernatural Council. We are here, where is everyone?"

Miller grunted, "About fucking time. We are taking shelter in the high school gym. I hope you brought back up."

The call ended and I pulled back to see whether he had hung up on me or my luck had just run out. The "service disconnected" light flashed.

Jerry increased the pace as best he could, weaving around the obstacles in the road. Mark navigated, having heard both sides of the conversation.

Ten minutes later, we pulled up to the high school, a modern building entirely fenced off with light teal wrought iron. A few dead zombies littered the lot as we parked.

"So, I guess I should have asked this sooner, but how does one kill a zombie?" Mark asked, taking careful stock of our surroundings.

"Head shot," I answered, checking the clips on my guns before tucking my blade back in its sheath at my back. Over the sheath I slipped two long blades. A girl could never have too many accessories.

Mark turned. "Seriously?"

"Seriously, or kill the necromancer, but I'd like to keep her alive if possible."

"I'm going to shift," Mark announced. "It feels less creepy to kill zombies as a wolf."

I shrugged. "Jerry, you want a gun?"

"I'd prefer a sword."

"Do you know how to use it?" I questioned, strapping throwing knives to my thigh.

"No more than a gun."

Mark grunted, "Stay between us."

"I'm not helpless," Jerry snapped.

Mark sighed, "No one said you were."

"It was implied," he seethed.

"Jerry! Get your head out of your ass. Mark and I are the better fighters. You are the only magic user. We will need you once we find the necromancer."

Jerry turned to glare at me and I handed over a spare dagger. "Don't hurt yourself with it."

With that he rolled his eyes and threw open his door, to my horror and Mark's. He stood there for one moment before the horde descended upon us. "SHIT!" he cried out.

Having opened his own door, Mark was throwing off clothing, his body hastily morphing from attractive male to pissed off wolf.

I pushed my own door open and slammed it behind me, pulling both guns. I was grateful Myrtle had talked me into the extra clip compartment sewn into the harness.

I shot two that were off to the side doing a slow shuffle to our location, being careful not to aim at Mark, who was fighting several with his massive paws. He was trying to keep the zombie filth out of his mouth. It wasn't working.

I took a step forward and Jerry yielded, stepping behind me as I took care of anything Mark missed, which wasn't much.

There were more than the original fifty-two from the graveyard. The bitch witch had been busy. A few were not human, although what race they were was beyond my knowledge. Probably something they picked up portal hopping.

We weaved through the high school, following the steady trail of zombies. I had emptied and replaced one clip already. Taking in the scene before me, I realized I might have underestimated my ammunition needs.

"Shit," I hissed.

Mark growled low in his throat padding next to me, in front of Jerry.

The necromancer and witch weren't in sight, but the original graveyard gang was beating mercilessly against the gym doors with slivers of glass windows. Decaying hands smashed against small sections of glass. The horde pushed forward, crushing their own kind in an attempt to feast upon living flesh.

Little known fact: while zombies are the true undead, you still have to feed them, massive amounts of live flesh. That's the primary reason no one fucking brings them back.

Well, no one of intelligence.

As one, the horde shifted, slowly, faces without eyes, mouths rotted away to reveal wasting teeth and the putrid stench of death.

"Lord have mercy," Jerry cried out, holding his nose.

Mark pawed my foot. "I know," I whispered.

"What does he want?"

"There isn't enough room here for us to take them all." I began pushing him behind me as I stepped carefully backwards, keeping my guns aimed. "We need space to kill all of them."

Jerry nodded once, his dark eyes nervously taking in the scene before him.

"No time like the present," I muttered, standing my ground as Jerry and Mark moved further back.

I was really wishing I had taken more blades.

The hallway was covered with floor to ceiling lockers, bright shiny paint soon to be marred with zombie guts.

Heaving a sigh I stopped, widened my stance, placed one foot slightly ahead and began taking head shots. If I had thought of it first, we should have placed bets. Two shots plowed into their intended targets.

Zombies as a species were not fearsome, but in large numbers they didn't stop, didn't rest, and didn't care about being hurt. They were the perfect soldiers, assuming, of course, one could keep them fed.

Where the fuck were that damn witch and necromancer? The witch might not be close by, but the necro had to be in order to give the command for the zombies to switch targets.

Cold dread settled into my stomach.

"Jerry, get Mark into the gym. Find the witch!" I screamed, stowing my guns and cleaving a path through the zombies for them with my twin blades.

"Hurry!" I urged them on, hoping I wasn't right.

My blades twisted and turned, faster than the blasted zombies, but a fucker still latched onto my shoulder, sinking his filthy teeth into my flesh.

With the guns I had reduced the mob in half. My swords reduced it further until only a few were left, including the asshole still attached to my shoulder. I had hoped he would dislodge with all my movements, but he was more aggressive than I guessed.

Flipping my blade around I struck behind me, meeting the soft flesh and bone of his stomach before wrenching the blade up and to the side. The weight of the zombie lifted as I cut his legs from under him. The teeth, however, continued to gnaw.

Disgusted, I slammed my back against the goo-covered lockers several times before he finally fell off. With a triumphant cry I hacked the head off and marched into the gym.

Had I not just fought with a zombie attached to my shoulder, I probably would have given the whole marching in without thinking thing a little more thought.

Instead, a blast of power had me dropping my sword and falling to my knees the moment I cleared the doors.

"Fucking witches!" I screamed.

Yep, I just revealed the witches to the general public. Oops.

"Well, well, well, who do we have here?" The robe gave her away as the witch, parading in front of me. "The legendary Executioner Olivia, trapped by the simplest of spells."

"I'm going to kill you," I informed the chestnut haired woman. She smiled, her brown eyes rich in swirling colors.

"How do you propose to do that?"

"You know, I'm not actually really particular on how it happens, just that it gets to be me."

She laughed again. That's just rude. She had obviously heard of me.

"Your mage," she continued, heavy disgust on that word, "was no match for me, either." She waved her hand over the limp forms of Jerry and Mark.

"Yeah well, we all have our bad days."

I took in the room. I know, a little fucking late for that decision.

The humans were huddled to the side, staying low to keep off the radar but watching with wary eyes. From my kneeling position, I could see that the children had been shoved against the far wall. The adults were trying their best to protect their small forms from the unknown danger. Steel replaced my features. Children are not to be harmed. Ever.

I swung my gaze to the other side of the gym, seeing the woman in white, also on her knees. Her robe was stained, the intricate silver thread designs pulled and ruined. Her hood was pulled back, revealing sunken eyes and silver hair. Her chin jutted out as her gaze remained riveted to the witch in front of me. Silver manacles circled her small wrists, connected by a delicate chain.

Her gaze fell equally hard on me. "You've killed my creations."

"I didn't have much of a choice."

She nodded, still unhappy. I was willing to bet freeing her would earn unneeded forgiveness.

"You pain in the ass witch, what the fuck are you up to?"

"Calling our makers," she answered with a flourish. She held her hands out, head tilted back, insane smile on her lips.

"Uh, who are you claiming are your makers?"

"Why, the Fae, of course." She withdrew her arms, tucking her hands into the wide sleeves of her robe.

I groaned. "Why in the seven hells would you think the Fae are your makers? Please don't tell me you believe the legend that witches are the result of a breeding experiment between the Fae and humans?"

The witch narrowed her eyes at me, her jaw clenching. "How dare you defile our heritage!"

"Great, now it's an insane witch I have to deal with."

Jerry stirred from the pile of arms and legs he and Mark had fallen in. I glued my eyes to the super bitch, trying not to give him away.

"You've clearly never met the Fae," I taunted.

Her eyes riveted to me, a small smile played over her lips. "You have?" Her voice had gone breathless. Quickly she crossed the distance between us.

I swallowed my groan. "Yes."

"How? When? Who did you meet? How did you contact them? How?" she demanded, her eyes glassy with the mention of the Fae.

"It's a long story."

She sat down in front of me, her black satin robes swishing pristinely around her.

"Tell me everything," she commanded.

"Release the humans."

Intelligence sparked in her eyes as she calculated my request. As she tapped her fingers against her knee, I could practically see her make a decision. Straightening her posture, she turned with an evil smile to the captive necromancer.

"Darling, won't you be so kind as to have her and the mage taken to our home?"

The necromancer hissed, "I'm not your darling." Her jaw clenched. It appeared she was physically fighting the command.

"Oh dear, it appears the obedience spell is wearing off." She stood in a fluid movement, brushing off her butt before moving toward the necromancer with brutal intent.

She bent at the waist, whispering below my hearing. Jerry groaned, reaching up to hold his head. With a snap of her spine, the witch spoke four words that rendered him unconscious again.

Great.

"You know what, let's bring them all," the witch announced. I strained against the invisible bonds. She confidently stalked in front of me. "Don't worry Executioner, I'll leave the humans."

With an index finger against my forehead, she only had to utter one word to render me unconscious.

Fucking witches, I can't say it enough.

Chapter 12

My head was split in two, it had to be. There was no other explanation of the misery that regaining consciousness was causing me. Judging from the pain in my shoulder joints, I must have lost my arms along the way as well.

With a groan, I forced my dry lids open.

"Oh wonderful, the star is awake."

I groaned again. "Shut up, witch."

A slap rang out against my cheek, forcing my eyes closed again. My arms were bound above my head, my feet dangling on the concrete. Not unlike the vampires I had interrogated and killed.

I opened my eyes with new vigor, seeing the necromancer in a dirty pile of blankets, resting against a stone wall. From the high, small window, I was guessing we were underground.

Fucking hell, I had about had it with basement torture.

Turning my attention to the bitch whose expiration date had come to my gleeful attention, my green eyes hardened.

"Keep it up and you will beg for death."

She slapped the other cheek and I got to see Jerry and Mark tied to chairs.

"Yes, we can't have them escaping from their restraints like you did with Nari."

"Remind me who that was again?" I knew the answer. He was a crazed demigod taking vampires and shifters, making them insane before playing with them. The deranged asshole was hard to forget. Was there some bad guy club where fuckers commiserated about my escapes from them?

She huffed before moving back behind the sparkling tray filled with gleaming torture devices. I grunted, lifting my head back up. If this bitch thought this was the first time I'd had my flesh sliced and diced, she was in for a surprise.

"Now, you will refer to me as Destiny when you beg for me to stop."

I laughed. Jerry and Mark didn't share my mirth.

"Stripper name?"

Her eyes narrowed at me, her hand coming to rest on a wickedly curved blade used for skinning animals.

"Right to the good stuff?" I continued to taunt.

Closing her eyes, she drew a long breath, hands lifted and elbows bent. I was fairly certain I had seen Kass do the same move in her prenatal yoga videos. She exhaled, releasing her shoulder as she did, smiling yet again.

"Now, that's better." Her hand slid to a small knife, handling the blade with confidence.

She approached Jerry with the same calm and cheerful demeanor.

"Jerry Abbot, you have quite the reputation in the magic community. Did you know, Executioner, he had a bounty on his head—until he showed up under your protection, that is."

"I didn't know that." I turned my face the best I could, watching Jerry's face shut down. Mark glared at him, their already turbulent relationship strained even further.

"It's not what you think, Olie," Jerry stated darkly, watching Destiny closely.

"You know what Jerry, after I get done killing this bitch, you and I are going to have a long fucking heart to heart. Whether that's before or after Mark says his piece, I'll leave that up to him."

Mark's eyes flicked to mine. He nodded his thanks before turning back to our more pressing problems.

Destiny laughed a soft, throaty sound. "Your confidence is unparalleled. I haven't had a specimen so undaunted by being restrained."

"This isn't my first rodeo. Why did Jerry have a bounty on his head?"

"Oh dear, I think I will let him tell you that. Jerry, if you please."

"No."

Destiny closed the distance between our bodies, taking no time to slide the blade down my left side over my ribs.

"FUCK!" Biting down on the pain, I tipped my head back, breathing shallowly.

Jerry was painfully silent.

"Tell her," Mark warned in low tones.

"I'm so sorry, Olivia," Jerry whispered.

Another precise cut split the skin on my right side. I whimpered, taking shallow breaths. Destiny pulled the blade back, my blood coating the fine metal. She looked at Jerry expectantly, the back of her head facing me.

"We're waiting." Her voice was soft, as though she wasn't carving me up because Jerry wasn't answering her questions.

"They will need the back story," Jerry grunted.

Destiny moved away from me, cleaning the blade before setting it gently into its proper place.

Waving her arm, she encouraged, "Please continue."

Leaning my head against my arm, I let my body sag, braiding the pain down deep.

With a reluctant sigh, Jerry began softly. "The first thing you need to know is that witches gather and gain power by taking it. Our power is not a skill level we are born with. The only way to advance from witch, to mage, to magician is to steal."

I didn't fucking know that. How had I missed that? That was HUGE. I suppose my knowledge of the other Supernatural beings wasn't as extensive as I would like to believe.

I looked away from him and back to the stone ceiling.

Jerry sighed, resigned. "Needless to say, then, I've earned my position as Mage by taking power from others."

Destiny tsked, "You are leaving out the best part. Tell them whom you took it from." Her voice hardened on the command.

"Everyone," Jerry responded.

"Everyone weaker!" Destiny yelled.

Jerry gave no response.

"How many families did you ruin? You didn't have to kill them all!" Destiny was livid, clutching a wide knife in her hand until her knuckles whitened amidst her tan skin. "You didn't have to kill them," she sobbed.

Throwing the knife down, she stomped out of the basement and out of sight.

I said nothing, still staring at the dark stone above me.

"How many?" Mark asked.

Jerry was silent.

"How many?" Mark roared.

"I lost count." Jerry admitted. "You don't understand."

"Help me to," Mark begged. Like me, he wanted there to be more to the story. We wanted Jerry not to be the heartless killer Destiny portrayed him as.

"We have more pressing problems," the necromancer cut in. "How do you plan to survive this?"

I grunted. She was right.

Closing my eyes, I pushed the pain in my ribs down again, hating how much energy I was wasting on the task. "Do you know where we are?"

"No, I've been blindfolded."

"I'm assuming you tried screaming for help?"

"While I'm not proud to admit it, yes I did." The softness of her voice had me cutting a glance her way. The regretful way she held her head was telling.

"The good news is we left a whole gym full of witnesses who can report back to Grams."

"Grams, this is your handler?" the necro asked.

"Correct."

She nodded thoughtfully.

"The containment spell she placed on the gym will not be broken until the next dawn."

I groaned. "So we are on our own. How did you get trapped? I thought necromancers were innately powerful."

The silver haired woman hung her head, "We are, but I was lonely and Destiny was..." She faltered, searching for the right word.

"Kind and available," I finished for her.

She nodded, meeting my gaze.

A door slamming above our heads had everyone shutting up and looking up, waiting. Destiny's heels clicked against the wooden steps leading down, and while the stairwell blocked us from watching her progress, we all tracked it by the sound.

She was smiling again, carrying five dark strips of cloth, each four inches wide.

"Since I don't have the time I'd like to properly torture you, we will have to move forward this way." She sounded resigned, put off that her torture would have to wait.

"You aren't strong enough to spell those," Jerry enlightened her.

She laughed, laying the dark pieces of fabric down. "I don't have to be."

"Jaelle, come here," Destiny commanded.

The necromancer's chain rattled as she stood to her full height, looking down at the smaller woman. "Don't be difficult, darling," she chided as Jaelle fought the command. "Enchant these five blindfolds with the shared memory spell."

Jerry pulled at his bonds. I sure as shit had no idea what was going on, but based on Jerry's attempt to escape right in front of our captor it wasn't good. Or perhaps the memory of his that she wanted us all to see wasn't good. It was hard to determine his motive.

With a few soft words and a silver glow, Jaelle complied.

Destiny tied the blindfold on her first before shoving her back to the soiled blankets. Jaelle landed in a heap, declaring, "You will regret your treatment of me."

"Not while you are spelled and bound," Destiny countered. Cocky bitch.

I was next, stiffening at her close proximity and unknown magic. I pulled back only to get slapped across the face. "Difficult," she hissed at me.

I smiled as she tied the offending fabric behind my head. "I try."

That earned me another slap across my open side wound.

I didn't enjoy having one of my senses cut off, and I strained to hear what was happening.

"There, now we can really begin. Jerry, reveal to me your kills."

I plunged downward, my vision blackened as I hitched a ride on memories that weren't mine. Looking out through eyes that didn't belong to me, I could no longer feel my body, but I felt anticipation at gaining my sweet revenge.

My head tilted down and I took in my reflection against the darkened glass where he waited for me. The only man who ever cared. The only one who came when the rest abandoned me. I didn't care that his soul was black and that he was using me to further his own agenda. He offered revenge and vengeance, for my family that was taken from me by a brutal murderer.

Clenching my fist, I used my other hand to push the silver reflective aviator glasses back up my nose, the sweat from the midday heat causing them to slide.

I was rewarded for my patience in the sweltering heat, watching the teenager flounce down the stairs in her teal dress, laughing with her friends who waved goodbye before she headed to the empty gym. The same place she went every Thursday to meet her pathetic excuse of a boyfriend. I smiled, knowing exactly what she would find.

The scene changed and Jerry's dark hands were wound against the teenager's neck, pulling not only the subtle magic into his body but also her life force, binding the two together.

"Excellent, Jerry," his mentor crooned, excited and aroused by Jerry's skill and ruthlessness.

We left behind the gym for a darkened forest where we followed prey larger than ourselves. Stealth was our ally. Our magic wasn't strong enough to confront him head on, yet.

Around another corner I peeked over my shoulder seeing no one else on the path. Making my move, I sprinted on silent feet, jumping onto the giant's back and wrenching, as quickly as possible mingling the two powers of life force and magic into my own body. Taken by surprise, the giant had no time to throw up his shields.

The faces flashed by one after another, after another, until we looked down to the last. Our mentor.

"Jerry, you don't' have to do this."

"I do."

"I did it to help you."

"You killed everyone I loved, and turned me into a murderer with their souls locked within me! Trapped forever inside of me!" I screamed, horror over what I had become finally sinking in. "You used me in your own sick and twisted game." Lowering my face next to his I whispered "Don't worry, I won't take your soul. I'm done with that." With one swift pull I took his massive power, merging it with my own before thrusting the dagger into his heart.

Jerry was screaming in real time. I jerked against my bonds at the sound. That was a lot to take in.

"Heartless bastard," Destiny whispered. "That was my father!"

Rapid breathing punctuated the silence before Destiny barked out her next command.

"Olivia, show me all you know about the Fae."

No, no, no, I whispered, not sure if the words were making it past my lips as I was flung into a memory I had buried down deep.

Chomping on my gum, I watched Six lecturing at the board. "The Fae are powerful magic users. Their ground game leaves much to be desired, but not many can get close enough to utilize that advantage."

Seven scoffed next to me, "Like, no one." I turned, looking at her fire red hair. "It's a fucking suicide mission," she informed me yet again.

I shrugged my sixteen-year-old shoulders, not giving a fuck. The door opened to our classroom, Six freezing in front as my Lord Master entered the room. Disgust clawed at my gut, but I hid it, kept it all hidden under layers of false sexual desire.

"Come with me," he said, laying a hand against my calf. My feet were propped up on the white desk in front of me.

With a carefree smile I slid out of my seat. "See you all on the flip side," I called out, not sparing a look behind me as I followed my Lord Master. The fucker probably wanted a quickie before I got sent to certain death.

The door to his room slid open and I followed him to where I shouldn't be, but we had broken this rule often enough. The smooth metal sliding home had my hands wanting to ball up and kill him. I fought the urge. Soon, but not yet.

He came at me with a growl, pinning my body against the wall before making short work of our clothing. Passion, that's what the books in the library called it. Exhausting acting is what I called it. The fool always bought it, though, or rather didn't give a fuck as long as he was getting off, repeatedly. I'm certain my performance wouldn't have fooled a more observant bed partner.

Getting dressed, I changed from my jeans into working leathers, pulling a slim vest over my dark shirt. Lord Master watched me, still sitting naked on the bed. "They aren't letting me come with you."

"I know," I answered softly.

He might have been a rapist, but he was my rapist and he worried after me, protected me from being passed around. It wasn't much, but I would take it.

"They are up to something."

Tying my dark blond hair back, I shrugged. "When aren't they?"

He scowled. "Selena shouldn't be sending you in. There are plenty of other flunkies she can sacrifice."

"You heard her," I reminded him, strapping on my throwing knives to my upper thigh, "she has to prove her methods work, prove I am all that she boasts."

Lord Master scoffed, "It's dangerous and untried. There's a reason no one has ever gone after the Fae."

I didn't disagree, but I was done getting dressed. If the Fae killed me now, so be it. I couldn't honestly say I cared. Seven would be pissed at our thwarted escape plan, though.

"Are you seeing me off?" I asked, standing in front of the door.

He shook his head, turning away. I walked out into the dark hallway, making my way to operations. No one stopped me. Though I was a lone trainee wandering the halls by herself, people knew me. Knew my killing reputation, knew the son of a bitch I was tethered to. Knew I was the leading experiment in my group. They gave me a wide berth.

The operations door slid open the same way the Lord Master's did and I took my place against the wall as the General debated strategy. His dark skin glowed with an eerie blueish haze in the darkened room as they went over their plan.

He watched me against the wall, his eyes roving over my body with interest, followed immediately by guilt. He didn't like my Lord Master. He called him a pedophile on more than one occasion. I still hadn't figured out what that word meant. Selena had just laughed.

"Four," Selena purred, "please come here."

Her voice was soft and gentle, but I knew better. Madness beat within her skull.

I nodded, saying nothing as I came to stand between her and the dark-skinned General. Selena might be crazy, but she was observant, watching her General's interest in me. I looked over the maps in front of me. She made a soft tsking sound before turning to the information in front of us.

"Tell us what you see," Selena commanded, her voice hardening.

I blinked, taking a second and third look, disappointed as I looked up at her. "These are of the human's home, not of the Fae lands."

"Very good, why does that upset you?"

"I'm walking in blind."

Selena nodded, her eyes on the General behind me. "Go back to the wall," her voice clipped. I removed myself from the path of her wrath.

"If this mission fails, gentlemen, I want you to know I will personally collect your heads."

They all stilled, properly terrified. "Now, let's be off."

Hurry this along. Destiny's voice rushed my ears.

I was screaming as pain blasted my senses apart, my body in pieces as I was sucked into the portal. The fucking Fae knew we were coming. The damn thing opened and everything was being drawn into its inky darkness.

I landed with a thud in the desert, looking around. Many of the generals had not landed well. At least they were spared from this heat. As I rolled to my knees, sweat trickled down my legs and fire burned the back of my neck. Selena stood, wary.

"We need to go for cover," I said, moving toward her and taking her hand, pulling her to the trees I could see in the distance.

"We were sold out," she hissed at me.

"I know, but we need to figure out a way home first."

The trees up ahead shook and stood, drawing toward us. "Fuck," I hissed, bracing for an attack.

The lumbering giants were in no hurry, and on the plus side provided much needed respite from the sun.

"Selena," a merry voice called out.

I looked high into the branches before turning behind me. The desert was gone, replaced by the growth of a lush forest.

A short man, thin with dark, olive-brown skin, stood behind us.

"I do believe you were warned of coming back," he called out in a singsong voice.

"Bob," Selena acknowledged reluctantly.

"Now, what is the price of this trespass?" Bob continued speaking, pacing in front of us. He stopped, his round eyes lighting up. "I know, your most valuable possession."

Selena grunted, "Fine, just send me back home."

Bob laughed, snapping his hands. Selena was gone. He laughed again. "Just wait until she finds out home doesn't mean the compound."

Bob's large eyes met my own terrified ones. "I am truly sorry for what is about to befall you."

The trees reached down for me, snagging my limbs and drawing me horizontal. It was a vulnerable position, one I hated. Voices filtered through the trees,

"I hear you found a trespasser."

"Do let me have a go at her, it's been ages."

"Get in line."

I tried to keep the panic at bay. Torture wasn't new, pain wasn't an unknown sensation. I could survive it, but for what? I had no way of getting home, no way of getting help. I was trapped here forever.

The first one stood next to me, his cloak so far forward I couldn't see his face, just two red pools where I assumed his eyes were. My skin caught on fire.

It was days of torture, days and weeks of pain beyond anything I had ever known. They took me to the edge in turns, passing my body around for hours until I was only searing sensations. They cut me apart only to put me back together, bled me out, fucked me, until finally I was broken.

Bob came to me then. "Go home, your father has great expectations for you," he said with a touch on my shoulder and sympathy in his voice. Then I was back on Lord Master's bed.

I was screaming as I regained consciousness in the basement, my eyes still covered. I thrashed against the bonds on my wrists, warm blood leaking down my forearms.

Destiny ripped my blindfold off, fear in her brown eyes, her breathing elevated. I was so caught up in my own misery I didn't immediately see the shifter standing behind her.

"What did you see?" he asked, his silver hair given a harsh yellow glow by the basement lighting. He had adopted a relaxed posture, hands in his pockets, leaning against the stone.

Destiny turned from me, shaking her head. "Bob," she muttered, moving back behind her shiny tools, giving them a sick look before turning to face him. "We want to contact Bob."

The shifter nodded before tilting his head up. "We've got company. Go." He shoved her. I tried to track where, but my mind was having a hard time not shutting down.

I could hear the skidding tires followed by a door being kicked in. "Down here!" I screamed, noting the raw taste of my voice.

Heavy footsteps pounded down the stairs as Logan and Darren appeared.

I nodded, closing my eyes. "Shifter magic." I'd never been so grateful for their ability to track each other. Turning my face into my arm, I pulled my emotions down deep.

Logan came to stand before me. Wrapping an arm around my waist, he ripped down the lumber I was tied to.

"Show off," I muttered, hiding my face in his shoulder.

My arms flopped down, circulation painfully returning. Logan eased me to the ground.

I huffed, putting pressure on my side.

"What happened, Olie?" he asked.

"Oh ya know, just making new friends," I grunted.

Chapter 13

Jerry took Jaelle back to the witch's store in town in order to free her from the chains.

Logan had offered to handle the humans in town, but I thought it would go a long way for me to show up. If nothing else, my bandaged side and swollen face would hopefully dull the complaints I knew were coming.

I walked through the gym with the terrified humans all staring openly at my battle worn self.

Great, another town hall style meeting. Let's hope everyone wanted to play nice this time. At least Logan was a comforting presence behind me. His hand resting on the base my neck would normally irritate me, but right now I needed the help staying upright.

I braced myself to speak with the terrified humans. "They were too scared to leave," Logan whispered, leaning closer to me.

"How long was I gone for?"

"Two days."

I nodded, rubbing my forehead. "Do you want the truth or do you want me to ease your fears?" I asked softly to the eyes trained on me.

Daniels took a shaky step forward, putting on a brave face. "The truth. We've seen—we know—" he fought to form a sentence.

I nodded. "There is far more that goes bump in the night aside from vampires and shifters. They are just the most prevalent. What you encountered tonight was a small fraction of our kind. A witch, a necromancer and her zombie horde. But knowing what they are won't make you feel better. These beings have always existed. In the past we'd have vampires wipe your memories, but now we're trying to be honest.

"What will make you feel better is that the zombies are dead and the necromancer freed. She will be a powerful ally in tracking down the witch who is responsible for this." My face hardened. "We are the barrier between humans and the evils of our world. We will never allow our kind to harm yours, and if they do, they will never pull a breath again."

Logan moved closer to me. Alright, so vampires didn't breathe, minor detail.

"I know that isn't enough to ease your fear of what you have seen, but this is the best I can offer." Something in my face or my raw honesty hit a nerve; Daniels cleared his throat.

"We've been talking and we don't want to become freak central—no offense, but we are going to call this a bomb scare."

I nodded, it would be for the best.

"Our reports will indicate the same." Logan's deep voice washed over me, infusing calm.

I nodded once more before turning away.

Logan drove me back to St. Ann in my SUV. Mark, Darren and Jerry took Logan's car—ha, good luck keeping your clothes magically pressed in that backseat, Jerry. Jaelle had her own transportation after she left the witch's shop, freed.

I sat in the passenger seat, curled up into myself.

We rode in peaceful silence for a while, my mind replaying the horrors Destiny had forced me to remember. Every so often, a tear would slip down my cheek.

"Do you want to talk about it?" Logan asked softly.

"No," I answered, turning to him. "Let's talk about the wedding."

Logan groaned, throwing me a gentle smile. He would hear about it from Mark. For now, a little distraction was needed.

"Lorraine wants private dance lessons from you."

I shrugged. "Sure, you want to learn the tango?"

He shook his head. "I have moves."

I laughed earnestly and while he didn't look at me I saw the crinkling of the corner of his eye, smiling at me.

"I'll organize it."

"We need to talk about centerpieces," Logan continued. "She wants these tall vases with twigs. Who the hell wants twigs as centerpieces?"

I laughed again. "What about mason jars with flowers?"

Logan did look at me now. "I discovered Pinterest," I admitted.

"I like it."

"Did we decide on a venue?" I asked, snuggling in the seat, exhaustion finally taking its toll.

Logan shifted. "She wanted to get married where Blake did, but now that it's been done she wants something better, something different, something more."

I groaned. "That's going to eat up the majority of the budget."

"I'm aware."

"Don't you have a cabin somewhere remote? I thought I heard Darren talking about it."

"Yeah, actually we do."

"Would it hold everyone?"

Logan silently debated, turning onto the interstate before shaking his head. "No, not the hundreds of people she wants to invite."

I nodded, shifting my body so my head rested on the console. I'll never admit it, but I wanted to be closer to Logan. I wanted to be closer to his warmth and the illusion of safety.

"Get some rest," he commanded.

Tentatively, he rested a hand on my shoulder. I laid my fingertips over his, biting back the tears. Damn shifter could probably scent all of my pathetic emotions.

Chapter 14

"Where do you want me to drop you off, Olie?"

I groaned, blinking in the daylight that robbed me of my vision.

"Ugh, manor I guess."

"Well, we're here, then."

"Oh, thanks."

Logan waited a moment before continuing on, "I cleared our dance lessons with Rose at Kitten for the day after tomorrow. I hope you don't mind."

I yawned, shifting my stiff shoulders. "Okay."

He nodded. "Are you going to be okay? It was the only opening they had."

I laughed, giving him a playful shove. "I'll be fine, Logan." It sounded like a lie to me, too, but he left me to my own delusions.

...

The first thing I did, once I had slept like the dead and eaten my weight in grilled cheese, was to send over three books I thought would help Lorraine. I didn't like her, but if she really was going to marry Logan, maybe a bit of information would help her.

I was setting up at Kitten when they arrived.

"Hello, and welcome to Olie's personal dance class," I joked.

Logan laughed, heading to the bathroom to change out of his work clothing.

Alone with Lorraine I asked, "Did you read the books I sent over?"

"No," she replied, checking her dark hair for split ends. "It was boring." I was going to split her head open.

That woman could shock me, constantly, which was why my mouth was once again hanging open, dumbfounded. "I don't give a shit if they are boring, if you are going to marry into the supernatural community you have to understand each culture." The bitch could sure try my patience.

"I'm not interested in their culture. I'll be their new Alpha. They should be interested in mine," she observed, checking her nail polish.

"Don't you think that respect goes both ways?" I asked, grinding my jaw.

She laughed. "I am going to be married to the most powerful shifter in the US. People already bend over backwards to be certain I am well taken care of. That trend will only be magnified once we are married," she finished regally.

"If you are going to be a good mate, you need to support your husband, not make his life harder," I ground out, losing my patience. "If he loses his title, it could come at the price of his life."

She shrugged. "That's his problem."

"So just to clarify," I expelled, my patience totally fried, "you will marry Logan for his title and power and then do nothing to help him with those burdens?"

"Yep," she said, stretching in her black pushup sports bra and matching shorts, "that about sums it up."

That sounded like a terrible deal. I wondered if Logan knew her master plan. Not my circus, not my monkeys, I reminded myself.

Logan came out, stalking across the dance floor. He had probably heard all of that. Blowing out a breath, I went to start the music, irritation steaming out of both our bodies.

Turning on the sweeping ballroom music, I sighed, lowering my shoulders and cracking my neck.

Forcing a smile on my lips, I turned to find Logan only a few feet behind me. I blinked rapidly, looking for Lorraine.

"She went to finish her reading," he growled out.

"Logan, if she doesn't want to, she doesn't want to," I informed him, moving into his waiting dance stance.

His hand rested comfortably against my hip. "I don't actually care what she wants," he declared, beginning to move without my direction.

Raising an eyebrow at him I asked, "You think you are good enough to lead?"

"Yep, you move easier."

"Move easier?"

He twirled me out and back, pulling me closer. "You aren't stiff."

I sighed, allowing him to lead and finding myself surprised at how much he actually knew. "I guess Lorraine needs some one on one lessons."

"Good luck with that." He looked down at me, his eyes resting on my lips. I was suddenly having flashbacks to pinning him against the dirty strip club wall.

I shrugged. "I just need to find the proper motivation." Looking up at him, my own eyes dipped to his lips. A moment passed after the song ended. "It doesn't appear that you need any lessons," I breathed, well aware of his warm hands still on me.

"No, it doesn't," he replied, just as softly. I broke the spell by moving away hurriedly to stop the music. I told myself I was not running away. His low chuckle disagreed.

…

Three days and a never-ending earful from Grams about the mess I had made in Madison later, I was sprawled on Tommy's floor, trying a first person shooter game. I was marginally better at it than the racing games, but not much.

"You kill people for a living, how are you this bad?" Tommy asked me, his fingers nimbly controlling his half of the screen.

"No idea," I groaned, setting the controller down.

Grams knocked lightly. "You have a minute?" Her eyes flashed to Tommy.

"I'm not a kid!" he yelled at my retreating back.

I followed Grams to her office. Not the time to fight that particular fight with him.

"Teenagers," Grams huffed, sitting behind her desk. Her computer monitor had been upgraded, I noticed.

"You aren't going to like this," she deadpanned.

"I gathered. Good news is I'm healed."

She nodded once. "Angelina's Master is requesting to meet the succubus that killed his son."

"Fucking hell, that doesn't bode well."

She shrugged in agreement. "Do you want to take backup?"

"Where is it?"

"The Centennial House."

I rubbed the back of my neck. "No, I can't take any. They'd view it as a sign of weakness and I'd need a damn army at their House."

"If you don't come back, I'm grounding Tommy."

"Fair enough."

"I heard that!" Tommy yelled from behind the door that we had neglected to close.

…

The Centennial House was immaculate. Armed guards escorted me to a formal meeting room with a heavy wood table. I certainly wasn't the last to arrive, but they made me wait, a stupid power play.

Good thing I now had Pinterest.

A half hour later, both double doors were thrown wide by a short vampire. He moved quickly to the side and a tall, olive skinned man glided in behind him.

"Olivia."

I nodded, not actually knowing his name.

"Zachariah," he introduced himself.

I nodded again, watching his progress. He sat across from me while the short man took up a post behind his right shoulder.

"You have quite the business here," he began.

I didn't say a word. It's always best to assume Master Vampires are trying to either fuck you or kill you. It's been a fair assessment in my life.

"No small talk?" he tried, smiling. The gesture didn't fit on his handsome face, nor did it reach his black eyes.

"Just say it," I offered softly.

The pretense drained from him, leaving an impressively scary vampire. If I hadn't had my Fae memories dredged up recently, I might have felt a glimmer of fear. As it was I was just tired.

"You have taken from me and you will pay."

I smiled. "I know." Probably not my best idea pissing off another Master Vampire, but I did.

He slammed his hands against the table, standing. "I trust you can see yourself out."

He didn't wait for my answer.

I groaned, leaned back, steepled my fingers and wondered, chances on leaving alive? I was a betting woman.

I wasn't expecting Angelina to walk through the doors, still open from Zachariah's hasty retreat.

"May I talk to you in private?" Angelina asked, closing the door behind her. Her jet black hair was shaped into an elegant knot.

"Fine," I grunted, anger infusing my previously tired body.

I hated the bitch. I was perfectly able to admit it was because she had what I wanted. But was it really her fault? I mean certainly, the timing of it was terrible, and I had killed her nest mate Gregory when he tried to beat Blake into marrying her, but wasn't the truth of the matter that she was just better than me?

Self-hatred is a beast willing to believe any lie.

I sighed, "Cut to the chase."

"Since I am Blake's mate," she said, placing heavy emphasis on mate, "I feel it is time to call in his favor." Her eyes danced with dark glee and I was certain we had that psychotic look in common.

"Favor?" I asked, racking my brain.

Angelina's gaze never left my own. "From the incident at Flame, with Lorraine and Wanda."

"To think, I had almost forgotten about that," I muttered. "Good thing you vamps have such exceptional memories." As vampires had proven previously, they were expert political tricksters and she was right, she could call in my favor. Bitch.

"You are to retrieve Blake's niece from a rogue band of vampires calling themselves the Liberators," Angelina said. "They are the ones who are attacking us and your manor."

"Done. Where are they?" I asked. I probably agreed to that too easily, but I wanted Patricia Bellarosa.

"It's more complicated than that, Olie. This niece, Brooke, willingly aligned herself with them. I want a guarantee they will not come after her or us," she dictated.

"You want me to eliminate the entire House?"

She shrugged, blanking her face out impressively. "Whatever you think will be best to adhere to my guarantee."

Bitch was clever. I wanted Patricia and I could go after her rightly, but her entire House? Probably not. If I did this, we would forever have this secret between us. I could see it coming back to haunt me. But dead men tell no tales.

"Now if you will excuse me," I forced out, "I have things to do."

"Wait," she called to my back.

I paused but didn't turn, trying to hide my wince at the sound of, "Aren't you going to offer your congratulations?"

Closing my eyes for a painful moment, I bowed my head, not looking back as I left. Politics be damned, I wasn't playing that bitch's game.

Mal found me on the stairs and raced up next to me. "You don't want to see Blake?" she asked.

"Nope," I answered, pushing out into the afternoon sun.

"Olivia, he needs you," she said, frustrated.

I laughed. "Nope," I said, and made my way to my car.

"Olivia!" She spun me around, casting a glance around at the other cars. "They are falling apart," she whispered. "I don't know all the details, but whatever is eating at them is spreading to the whole House."

Cold seeped into my heart, numbing my emotions and shutting down my give-a-shit center. "Then transfer Houses, Mal, it's not your job to clean up after them." I turned back toward the SUV.

I knew transferring Houses was a terrible idea. Tate, while currently not able to handle his shit, was a fair and just leader and since vampires were powerless to disobey their Masters, a transfer would leave Mal vulnerable. I was an asshole.

I turned to Mal. "I'm sorry Mal, but I can't help them. They've chosen their side."

"They chose wrong," she whispered, lines being drawn between us, our friendship being overridden by vampire politics.

I shook my head. "It's been a pleasure, Mal."

I turned and left with that, neither of us speaking the obvious. I wasn't welcome anymore and I didn't care.

Chapter 15

Annoyed with myself and the whole fucking situation, I went to blow off steam at Sonny's Gym.

I liked it there. No one bothered me, no one asked if I needed help, and Sonny let me work out after hours, when he conducted his more dangerous business.

It was one of those nights. He was waiting on a client when he found me doing pull ups on the raw pipe until my palms bled.

He blew out cigar smoke with a long exhale as I threw my knees over the bar, moving into crunches. Still he watched me.

Finally, I flipped to the ground, gulping down water and air.

"You do realize working out this hard won't be creating muscle as fast as you're destroying it?" he asked.

I shrugged. "I trained this way the first fifteen years of my life."

"Where was that at?" he questioned.

"Hell," I answered, pulling myself back up for more.

Sonny shook his head, pointing his cigar at me. "You are self-punishing. You did something and think beating the shit out of your body will make you feel better."

I dropped back down, smiling at Sonny. "It's not what I did. It's just who I am that isn't good enough," I clarified for him.

The door opened and he shut his mouth, turning to meet with his client.

I went back to assaulting my body.

I wasn't paying attention to the crowd up front. Their energy was hostile and borderline beast, which was what Sonny specialized in. He had the unique ability to help those close to the edge come back. Unfortunately, that also meant he knew instantly if said shifter was too far gone, and no one ever wanted that news.

"Olivia, can you come here please?" Sonny politely called out to me. Huh, that got my curiosity piqued. I weaved between the bags, my body close to shutting down from exhaustion, to see who was out there.

"Bear?" I questioned. His eyes were darkly colored with the power of his shifter. I wasn't sure if it was his shifter or him that was trying to launch himself from his captor's hands at me.

"He needs a sparring partner, Olivia," Sonny stated, chewing on his cigar, all business. He stared worriedly at the large shifter.

"Done," I answered easily. I needed to see if I was strong enough to go after a House of vampires.

"Put him in the ring. The magic will help him," Sonny instructed.

"How did he get this way?" I asked, sliding into the ring with Bear.

"Someone drugged him," grunted the man helping to push him into the ring.

"With what?" I asked, not having seen this before.

"Shit if we know," the man said, rubbing his face wearily as he released Bear.

Bear lumbered forward, taking a few uncertain steps before his gaze locked onto me.

"Come on sweetheart," I taunted.

Bear's muscles rippled under his skin, talons sprouting from his fingers. I huffed. I really wanted talons. It would completely eliminate my need to keep daggers and knives hidden on my person.

He came at me fast, throwing sloppy punches, which was very unlike Bear. The man could handle himself expertly. I wondered what else the drug was doing to his body.

"Sonny, call Jerry," I said, easily dodging the right hook to my chin and landing a solid kick to his midsection.

I was rewarded with an "oof," a shake of his head, and a slight staggering. He held himself upright on the ropes, his breathing labored.

"Bear, can you hear me?" I asked, moving out of my fighting crouch to take a tentative step closer.

He growled, shaking his hairless head again before lowering it and rushing me. Easily, I skirted to the side, watching him tangle in the ropes.

"Jerry is fifteen minutes out," Sonny declared, hanging over the ropes, cigar hanging out of his mouth as he watched us closely.

Bear untangled himself, heaving up with a growl, his body wanting to shift but the magic in the ring keeping him in check.

"Where were you guys tonight?" I asked, moving under Bear's rapid-fire punches.

"Halfling," Bear's friend offered.

"The new human and supernatural mixer club?"

"We had a few complaints about witches screwing with the humans and were checking it out," his friend admitted.

"Why where you checking it out, don't they have their own security?"

I turned to look down at Bear's friend, who shrugged under his leather jacket, a red blush growing from his neck.

"I don't believe it's Caleb's place to divulge such information," Sonny stated. "Look out," he nonchalantly warned me. The air in my lungs vacated, my face bouncing against the mat, Bear's weight crushing me.

"Ouch." Reaching back, I made contact with the skin on his shoulder, letting meekness sink into our connection and into him. He wasn't having any of it. Pressing his face into my neck, he inhaled deeply and I felt his growing excitement.

So pushing wasn't going to work; pulling was my next trick. Steeling my nerves, I let my hand relax against his shoulder as I began pulling in the raging emotions under his skin. I pulled back with a yelp; what was happening under his skin was far beyond my abilities to soothe.

"Um, you might want to consider clearing the gym," I muttered, head-butting Bear before I flipped myself up.

"Oh," Sonny said, clearing his throat.

"I—I don't know—" said Caleb. "He's pretty out of control. He'd hate himself if he hurt you."

"He won't hurt me," I assured him.

Bear's beast charged and this time, I let him take me to the ground, his heavy weight supported by his arms.

"Either go or stay, but either way, this is happening," I warned.

I needed to get over Blake, and a distraction of mind-blowing sex was going to do the trick. At least that's what I was telling myself.

This will work. My eyes roved over him, appreciating his broad shoulders and thick arms.

His nostrils flared. He nuzzled the side of my neck. Dimly I heard the doors closing after Sonny and Caleb.

Bear's eyes traveled slowly over my face, taking in my elevated breathing and scenting my arousal.

"Olivia," his voice was lower, gravelly, and all animal.

"Bear," I answered.

Bear smiled, leaning down to my ear and licking the shell before he whispered, "I can smell you." Slipping a hand under his shirt, I pressed my fingers lightly against his abs, enjoying the feeling of his ragged breath.

I let my desire seep out, my raw need slipping down my arms into him. Bear closed his eyes, moving between my legs, pressing my hand flat against his stomach. "Can you feel me?" I whispered.

Bear's eyes opened and I watched his beast in control. I couldn't help leaning forward, my grin spreading as I tugged on the hair peeking above his waistband.

Bear wrapped his large hand around the soft flesh on the back of my neck. I was impressed by his control as he forced my head to tilt up. Slowly, he lowered his mouth to my own. Heat blasted through my veins and I pushed closer to him. My hand wrapped around his back to pull him near. His free hand pressed against my shoulder as he pulled away.

"Are you sure?" he whispered close to my ear, my body pressing against his massive erection.

"Yes," I whispered.

"You are done being in control, darling," he warned me, nipping at my neck. I lifted my chin, giving him access to the delicate skin there. He growled, biting down harder, and reached up to lock my hands above my head. Inhaling sharply, I arched my body against his, moaning.

"You want it, you have to take it," I warned him, my eyes darkening in lust.

Slowly, with a degree of control that surprised me, he removed my wraps, then began lifting up my black tank top, pressing kisses to my naked flesh, inch by slow inch.

I growled, thrusting my hips at him. He looked up at me, his tongue working small circles under my rib cage, my hands securely in his own above my head.

Another inch and he was wonderfully close to my bra. Releasing my hands, he removed the offending tank top, his warm hands sliding over my sides. Gently, he lowered the straps of my bra before unclipping the back and setting it to the side. With a slow kiss to my lips, he had my hands secure again. The cool air of the gym pebbled my nipples as a chill had me shivering.

Bear's warm lips enveloped my right nipple, drawing it into his soft mouth before his teeth rolled the delicate flesh painfully around. I wanted to run my hands into his scalp and draw him closer, but he wasn't letting them go. Instead, I cried out, arching my shoulders back.

He was an expert torturer, and I was a willing subject.

"I want to touch you," I whispered as his attention shifted to my other nipple.

"Mmmuhuh," he sounded, the vibrations sending painful tendrils of need straight to my groin.

"Bear," I warned as he continued his assault.

Moving my leg around his hip, I pressed my heated core against his growing length, desperate for a touch.

He growled lowly. "I didn't give you permission to do that."

I laughed softly, thrusting my hips before questioning, "Does that make you want to punish me?" My hips refused to stop.

He growled again, releasing my hands to forcefully grab handfuls of my ass, pressing me painfully against him. Lowering his face in my breasts, he nipped the tender flesh on each before rising to his knees, removing his weight. I pushed up on an elbow, wondering if he had come around and changed his mind.

Our clothing being torn off had me clamping my mouth closed with a smile.

He leaned back over me, beast and man breathing heavily as his gaze roved over my body. His fingers trailed a scorching path from my calf up my inner thigh before he pinned my hands above my head again.

Flesh on flesh contact had me widening my legs, hooking one around his hip in raw need.

"About time," I whispered, using my heel to push his hips down closer to me.

Tattoos swirled around his impressive muscles, flexing and bunching as he refused to release my hands. I had the distinct feeling he had an impressive bondage collection.

He shifted his hips up and I whimpered to his knowing smile.

I grunted my disapproval, wiggling to get free. Slowly, he used his free hand to toy with the folds between my legs.

"Bear," I groaned, fighting the restraint, which only made what he was doing that much hotter.

My head rolled on my shoulders as he tormented my clit with his thumb before sliding a finger into my waiting warmth.

I bucked, trying to press into his hand harder. His breathing was ragged as he pulled his hand out of me. "Do you need a safe word?" he asked seriously.

I shook my head, my hips still pushing for him. The mammoth covered my body with his own, forcing the air from my lungs as he pushed himself roughly inside of me.

I sucked in a deep breath, eyes closed as the room began to move. Bear moved us against the ropes. The cold material was a stark contrast to his warmth and I flinched closer to him. His hands supported my hips, his fingers digging in, creating a sweet combination of pain and pleasure. My head rocked back but I couldn't bring myself to care as he moved roughly inside of me, pushing out all traces of Blake and the gentleness we once had. I gave in to the force and the beautiful joining of pain and pleasure.

Bear's large member hit ever nerve in my body perfectly, driving me towards an explosive orgasm that rocked the very walls inside my body. He wouldn't relent, his speed increasing as I attempted to recover from my first orgasm, only to have my second thrust upon me as I cried out again, his speed increasing still.

Just when I thought I might have made a mistake about the safe word, as my third leg-numbing orgasm pummeled through me, he also roared out, stilling as he emptied into my body. Bowing my head onto his shoulder, I sucked air into my overheated body.

"Bear, are you alright?" I asked softly.

Slowly he lifted my face to his, in perfect control. "Olivia." My name was a strain on his lips and I struggled to get away from him.

"It was the easiest way to get you back."

"I could have hurt you." His eyes were angry, but he wasn't releasing me.

Reaching a hand to caress the stubble on his cheek, I shook my head. "But you didn't."

"Olivia," he marveled as I pulled my gaze back to his eyes, "you saved me."

"Aw, I bet you say that to all the girls."

A sudden pounding on the gym doors had Bear setting me down and pushing me behind him. I peeked around his broad shoulder when the doors burst open.

"Mark is looking for you, he said Jerry was kidnapped," yelled Caleb across the gym, averting his gaze from our naked forms.

"Fucker," I hissed, throwing on my shorts and tying the ruined sides together.

"Did he say where?" I asked, sorting through the clothing for my shirt. Bear handed it to me, slipping back into his unharmed jeans. My shirt wasn't so fortunate. I wrapped it under my arms before tying it behind me.

The young shifter looked at me with a glazed look in his eyes as I finished tying.

"Wow," he mouthed, impressed.

Slinging myself out of the ring, I closed the distance between us aggressively, slapping him sharply across the face. "What else did Mark say?" I demanded, forcing myself not to shake him.

He swallowed, blinking his intelligence back.

"Uh, that he thought they were going to succeed this time," he muttered.

My face paled with horror.

Bear was now paying attention, having leaped out of the ring to stand next to me. "What does that mean, Olivia?"

I shook my head, running to my bag and pulling my phone out. "If they succeed in reaching the Fae, we are all fucked," I whispered, true terror stealing my breath.

Six missed calls—dammit, I am a horrible friend and asshole. My phone couldn't respond fast enough as I called Mark back.

"Olie," Mark rasped.

"Where are you?"

"At home."

"I'm on my way. Mark, I will find him, I swear it."

"I—it's—just hurry." He ended the call, his voice broken and hopeless.

I turned to leave, only to be stopped by Bear's hand on my arm. "Call the Alpha and let him know where we are," he commanded Caleb.

Turning his attention to me, he paused, his eyes widening slightly before narrowing. "I can feel you."

"Good, then you know I am leaving." I pulled out of his grasp forcefully.

He was hot on my heels trotting down the hallway. "What does this mean, Olivia?"

"That we had consensual sex." I stomped down the stairs, the noise ending our conversation until we hit the parking garage.

Taking a look at Bear's worried face, I stopped to assure him, "Don't worry. It will fade and distance will eliminate it entirely, if it's too much for you."

My SUV blocked my view of him as I jumped around to the driver's side. I threw myself into the seat, smashing the gas pedal and roaring out of the parking lot. He hardly had time to close his door.

I couldn't help but feel this was all my fault. If I hadn't told Sonny to call Jerry, would I still be rushing over to Mark to figure out what the hell happened?

I remembered little of the drive as I swerved between cars, using the large size of my SUV to force others out of my way.

Squealing into Mark and Jerry's driveway I jolted to a stop, fear icing my stomach, my fingers tightening on the steering wheel.

Bear reached over, resting his fingertips on my forearm, my fear and worry clouding his face.

"I'm sorry, Bear. I should have warned you."

He squeezed my arm trying to reassure me. I looked over at him with tears in my eyes before I clamped down on my emotions, hissing out a breath.

I nodded my thanks before opening the car door.

Bear fell into step beside me as I strode with my hands flexed against my ruined clothing. I probably should have changed, but it was too late now. I pushed open the door, already ajar.

Mark sat wringing his hands together. He wanted to do something, anything, but he didn't know what the next step was. "Olie," he exhaled, standing as we entered. The loss in his eyes killed me. He was trying to keep it together. His jaw clenched, he was battling anger, at war with panic, his beast wanting to rip open everything around him.

I embraced him, holding him close. Pulling back, I gingerly touched the ghost of a blade mark on his neck. "Silver. They used you to get him quietly."

He nodded and I shifted my gaze to his brown eyes. "Tell me everything."

Mark blew out a breath, moving to sit again. Bear stayed by the door, watching outside to give us the illusion of privacy.

"It was that witch again and her flunkies, but they had help, they had shifters."

Bear turned from the door, eyebrows drawn tightly over his darkening eyes. The news of a shifter working with the witches was a personal betrayal to all shifters.

"How did they leave?" I whispered the question, afraid of the answer.

Mark's eyes darkened, his hopelessness echoing in me. "A portal."

I hung my head, wrenching my hands.

"They're gone, aren't they?" Mark whispered.

Determination steeled my spine as I drew my green-eyed gaze to him. "I will find him."

"How, Olivia? How can you track a portal?" Mark wailed. "I've lost him. I've failed him."

I moved without thinking, framing Mark's head with my hands, kneeling in front of him.

"I will find him. I'm going to see The Oracle."

"You will?" his beast backed down from pushing him into shifting, relief relaxing his shoulders.

I nodded solemnly, moving my hands to his shoulders, standing.

"Yes, I'm going to The Oracle."

Bear moved to my side, "The Alpha and Darren are here."

I nodded as I watched Mark's control solidify, hope giving him strength. A car door slamming had me turning to the front door, watching Logan and Darren run into the room with hurried movements. My gaze met Logan's.

"Olivia," Logan tried, casting a glance at Mark. Then both he and Darren scented the air, their eyes widening as they looked first to me, then Bear. Logan's neck reddened and his corded muscles flexed in his t-shirt with restrained power.

"Yeah," Bear said, rubbing the back of his grizzled neck, "it happened." He smiled, meeting my gaze.

I couldn't help answering the smile before I snapped back to the situation at hand. I didn't need to explain my actions to them, well, I guess I kind of did since it involved Bear being drugged. Whatever. This was not the place for it.

"I'm going," I announced to the room, making my way outside.

Logan and Darren shared a look before Darren nodded, moving to sit with Mark.

Bear looked at his Alpha and Logan shook his head ever so slightly. His irritation surprised me. Why did Logan care who I slept with?

"I can see you, fuckers. I'm doing this alone," I grunted, clearing the door and the porch steps and quickly heading to my SUV. I didn't typically feel awkward being half naked, but for some reason Logan was unnerving me. I refused to look too closely at that.

Before I managed to shut my door, Logan was putting on his seatbelt in the passenger seat. Fucker moved fast when pissed, good to remember.

I grunted, starting the vehicle and staring at him.

He shrugged, "You are not going to listen to me about not going. I need you alive for several reasons, and Bear would make my life difficult if something happened to you."

I broke my glare off to check traffic backing out of the driveway.

We drove in silence for a while before Logan finally asked, and I knew it was coming, "So Bear, huh?" Who I fucked was none of his business.

If I had to go meet with the banshee from hell, it wasn't a bad way to power up.

"Demon whore, Logan, don't tell me you forgot already."

Logan shifted in his seat, apparently not enjoying the reminder of how he had referred to me.

"That was before."

"Before what?" I asked, worry gnawing at me. Finding no use in this conversation, I took out my frustrations on my fingernail.

"Before you fought for a place by my side."

I laughed, I couldn't help it.

"Logan you do realize my help is temporary, right? That once you and Lorraine are married I will never sit beside you again in that capacity?"

He fidgeted again. "Yeah, about the wedding—Hey, do you know where you are going?" he asked as I made a sharp turn.

"Yes."

"You've been here before?" he asked, shocked.

I cast him a sidelong glance before flexing my shoulders back. "Yeah, part of being named lead Executioner is meeting and surviving The Oracle."

"I didn't know that."

"I'm not surprised," I snipped back. Shit, I didn't need to take my irritation out on Logan. I needed to get Jerry back to be sure he and Mark had a chance at happiness. My thoughts flittered to Blake and pain constricted my chest. Someone should get to be happy. I stomped the accelerator. They would be happy.

"We'll find him, although I think being drained by a vampire would be a safer alternative."

"It would be," I agreed, "but it won't work. I'm not connected to Jerry in the same way I was to your grandfather."

He nodded, digesting that as he turned to look out the window.

...

Old magic coated the small clearing in front of the sheer rock wall. Logan pulled off his shirt, tucking it into his waistband. I had my bag open, pulling on jeans and a teal shirt.

"You can't come with me," I announced, closing the back doors firmly.

"Bullshit."

"No, I'm serious, Logan." My gaze remained riveted to the gray rock laced with ribbons of pale purples and subtle blues.

He moved in front of me, clamping my forearms in his oversized paws. I forced my gaze to his caramel depths.

"Make me," the fucker taunted me.

I blinked at him. "Who are you, and what have you done with Logan the asshole?"

He shrugged, turning back to the wall.

"Change is in the air, Olie."

I eyed him warily as I shook out my arms. Sonny's advice about not pushing my body too hard was well warranted now. Blowing out a breath, I focused on the handholds in front of us, and began the long and painful ascent.

Logan grunted, his foot slipping. "I'm surprised this place isn't coveted by rock climbers."

"It's the magic. It hides itself from anyone who hasn't been here before."

"That's different."

"It's old, The Oracle is old magic."

"Unstable magic."

"That too," I agreed, "but for a price you can have all the answers you seek."

"What is the price?"

"Last time it was a memory."

"Of what?"

"I don't know anymore."

"Oh."

Surprisingly, I felt I should elaborate, should try to communicate with him. Maybe this really was a shifting in our relationship. "The Oracle is bound to the stone. Legend claims it was an Indian mystic who overstepped her power; others claim the stone came from overseas until it grew to this. Whatever the origins, it bores easily so with the memories it takes as payment, it finds entertainment. If you give too many of your memories, you never remember how to leave, until you are just a voice in the stone."

"Enchanting."

I wheezed, my foot slipping, a stone digging into my hip before I readjusted.

"You good?" he asked, breathing harder.

"Yeah."

My hands ached, tiny slices numbed my fingers, and an ache spread across my shoulders.

Logan passed an anchor with a bolt sticking out.

"Why aren't there more of these? This is a shitty climb."

"The Oracle doesn't like metal marring her face, plus I think she likes to see us struggle."

"I'm not looking forward to the return trip."

I groaned, "Agreed."

Pain was making my forearms shake so I tried to use my legs more, which only had my quads equally unstable.

"Almost there," I groaned, taking a risky handhold a little too far.

With a final groan, I slipped my hand over the flat entrance.

"Come on, big man," I grunted. After sliding my body over the edge, I turned around on my stomach, offering him a hand. With our hands clasped, I wiggled backwards on the dusty surface, bringing Logan with me.

He lay there on his stomach next to me, panting, okay actually we both were panting. "No wonder she doesn't get many visitors."

Huffing in agreement, I rolled to my back, flexing my fingers and staring up at the ceiling. I sighed when a face appeared, winked, and quickly disappeared.

Logan shifted his head, moving closer to me. "I saw a face in the wall," he whispered uncertainly.

"Me too, everything we say is now being listened to."

The rock around us rumbled in warning, "Best not keep The Oracle waiting." I rolled to my side before forcing myself to stand.

"I'd kill for a backrub," Logan grunted, using his shirt to wipe the sweat off his face.

I tried not to be distracted by his tan, muscular stomach. I was fairly unsuccessful, slamming my shoulder into the rock outcropping.

"Easy there, wandering eyes," he teased.

Scowling at him, I rubbed my shoulder as we moved deeper into the caves. Exterior daylight was nonexistent as we made our way by the artic glow given off by the rock, its power humming with excitement.

Down a twisted corridor we moved through the stone passage, more faces appearing and disappearing as we walked cautiously through.

"Can they harm us?" Logan asked quietly, his broad shoulder almost brushing the pitted rock face.

"They didn't last time I was here."

"Oh goody," an excited, high-pitched voice called from up ahead. "A repeat customer."

Logan growled, moving closer to my shoulder. I welcomed his warmth in this soul sucking cold as I fought back a shiver. "Here we go." Pushing my shoulders back, I straightened my spine, bracing myself to confront the insanity I knew was coming.

"Oh how sweet, you brought a pet, can I keep him?" a woman made of stone inquired, the jagged edges of her form rippling as she sat up from her fainting couch, also made of stone.

Logan pushed closer to me, pressing his shoulder into my back.

"We have come to ask a question, Oracle."

The stone woman crossed her arms. "Right to business. But I'm lonely," she pouted in a childlike voice. Standing, she moved toward Logan.

Moving him behind me, I blocked her path.

The stone face crumbled into a glower, The Oracle hissing, "Protect the pet, protect the change, protect the future."

That made no sense. Ignoring it, I kept my face impassive. She turned her head at impossible angles, watching me closely.

"FINE!" she screamed, the voices of many blending together, shaking the rock walls.

"What do you want?" She resumed her leisurely sprawl on the couch, feigning boredom.

"I need to know where to find a mage named Jerry and what date and time will be best to obtain him from said location."

The stone woman narrowed her eyes. "You've gotten smarter since last time."

I chose to ignore the comment. I didn't need to piss her off more.

"I want a memory from him," she pouted, stone sliding like water as she pointed an arm at Logan.

"I will give you the memory of his kiss," I offered softly, remembering Logan's lips on mine in the seedy strip club.

She sighed dejectedly. "Only his kiss? You offer nothing more? I want the feeling of his body against mine, of penetration, and of hearing his cries of bliss."

"I do not have those memories."

"I accept, payment first."

She reached forward and pulled me down next to her onto the cold stone. I felt the loss of heat from Logan, shivering as her stone arms surrounded me, freezing me to my core. Locking my eyes on Logan, I felt the memory pulled from my grasp.

Adrenaline spiked my blood as my body fought her pull, but she was powerful and I no match for her. Biting on my lip, I clenched my eyes closed against the cold pain in my brain while she extracted her price.

Memories flooded my mind: Logan's lips against mine, his total abandonment as he worked those twin lush mounds against my own, dragging his tongue across mine before pulling back. I remembered the sear of his warm hands pressing into my back before he lowered one to grab the firm flesh my ass, barely concealed in my stripper attire. My body remembered the feeling of his other hand nesting on the back of my neck, his fingers tangled in my hair.

The fleeting images vanished. "It's okay, Olivia," Logan comforted me. Opening my eyes, I found him kneeling in front of me. I wanted to touch him, wanted him to hold me. I wanted the comfort he offered.

The memory sucked me in again: his erection pressing against me, my body responding in kind, liquid heat pooling between my legs.

The stone bitch dropped her head onto my neck and a scream was forced out from my lips.

She chuckled, "That will do nicely."

"Here is your information." Her voice echoed in my rattled skull, grating against my nerve endings.

Jerry was bound and gagged, his usually clean white shirt dirty and wrinkled, his eyes wild as he watched someone I couldn't see. The scene shifted until I was seeing a street corner, Main and Becker. Another flash, and a calendar moved to the forefront: two days' time.

With a jolt I was back in control of my body. Logan dragged me away from the stone bitch. I let him, needing his heat desperately.

"Did you get it?" he asked, holding me closely.

I nodded.

"Don't you want to know about your reign as Alpha? Who you will mate? What your children shall be named?" The cold bitch crooned, "I can answer all."

"Are we done?" Logan asked me, staring coldly at The Oracle. I nodded and he helped me down the same twisting hallway.

"You have to rest before we go down."

I shook my head, "Two days, we have to get to Jerry in two days."

Logan held me close. "You won't be going anywhere if you fall."

I huffed out a laugh. "Too bad you can't fly." I grinned, my teeth chattering.

Idly he stoked my hair, thinking, drawing the same conclusion I was, probably.

"If I fall, don't catch me, just get to Jerry."

Logan's arms tightened around me but I pushed him away. While I longed to stay there in a faux sense of safety, I had a job to do and one rogue mage that needed saving.

"Let's go," I said, pushing myself away. I flexed my sore and shaking hands as I pulled my focus internally, not allowing anything but the task at hand to dominate my thoughts.

Since when did I think Logan's arms were safe? Seriously, The Oracle must have done more of a number on me than I realized.

Sitting down on the cold stone ledge, I pulled in another breath before flopping over to my stomach, trusting my foot to find traction. Beside me, Logan did the same, watching me closely.

I wanted to ask what memory she took, but I didn't need the distraction and I didn't care, I told myself. Yeah, I didn't believe that, either.

My left foot found purchase that felt secure under my boot.

"Here goes nothing."

Keeping my stance narrow I settled my right foot below my left, sliding my torso off the security of the cool stone. My shirt bunched with my movement, the cool breeze slicing through my skin, threatening to set off my shakes even further.

I gritted my teeth and forced my left foot down again. The pain was bearable, for now.

Logan moved his bulky form smoothly to my left, his descent quicker than my own. My fingers ached, the small cuts from earlier growing as the sharp stones shredded my flesh.

The wind buffeted us as we descended. My left hand gripped an easy hold as I went to move my foot farther down. My toe just nudged another, smaller hold. Pebbles dropping from my left hand had me ripping my attention back up, watching my handhold being pulled back into the stone.

"Motherfucker," I hissed. "Hurry up, Logan! Our time here has run out!"

We were only halfway down; a fall from here would still kill me. Possibly not the shifter, but I didn't want to test that theory.

Logan sent me a glance as I shifted my left hand, willing speed into my movements.

"What's happening?" he asked.

"My holds are disappearing, are yours?"

"No."

"Fucking Oracle, playing favorites. "

Another ten feet and I was braiding pain down, no time to rest, no time to recuperate. I could only gasp, grunt, and hurry as my handholds and footholds disappeared.

Logan had disappeared from my view and I chanced a look down, finding him almost directly beneath me.

"What are you doing?" I demanded.

"Saving your ass."

"What the fuck did I tell you?"

"You aren't the only one who has issues taking orders."

I grunted, couldn't argue that point.

My right hand slipped and at the same moment, both my footholds dissolved into the stony surface. I was left dangling, all my weight on my left hand.

My jaw clamped shut on the cry I wanted to let loose as my shoulder took the full weight of my body. The stone in front of my face shifted, smiled, and sucked in my last handhold. I scrambled, but I wasn't fast enough to combat the gravity that plucked greedily at my heels.

The rock face slipped quickly past my eyes, my feeble attempts to secure an additional hold ruined by my downward force and The Oracle's games. Just as suddenly as my fall began, it stopped, an uncomfortable force binding my shoulders back. Logan strained, his forearm tense against the wall, tendons bulging, fingers shifting into claws that sliced though the impenetrable stone like butter to hold us.

"Drop. Me."

"No," he hissed.

I reached my hand out to the nearest hold, watching it disappear into the rock with a pop.

"Let me go, Logan," I said more softly, looking awkwardly up at him. "One of us has to make it out of here, has to save Jerry and stop the witches."

I closed my eyes for a long moment. "Apparently that is you," I breathed out, the words leaving me empty.

As I met his raw sienna gaze again, emotions flittered through him, determination at the forefront, loss a close second, and pain. He was strained.

Reaching my hands up behind me at a twisted angle, I let my guards down, letting my power and acceptance flow into him, my knowledge that time was never my friend and this was always the inevitable conclusion.

His eyes widened and his grip tightened. Met with this resistance, I did the next best thing. The shirt moved roughly over my face, catching my chin and nose as it came off.

"OLIVIA!" Logan's roar shook the rock around us.

I could see him reaching down, still clutching the teal shirt, shock etched on his features. I was so focused on him that I saw the exact moment his expression changed to confusion before all the air was pushed from my lungs, the back of my head bouncing against a hard surface.

"Ow."

Blinking back the pain, I didn't dare move. There was no way I had reached the ground yet. Looking up, I saw Logan moving quickly, both hands turned into formidable claws as he made his own path down, leaving the stone scarred and marred where he passed. For once, I was content just watching the muscles in his back ripple and shift. The man was attractive, I had to give him that. With a jump, he cleared the last few feet, landing with his legs braced on either side of me.

Bending his knees, he kept his weight off me as he reached out, gently searching my head for any open wounds. He sat back on his heels and pushed out a relieved breath.

A face appeared next to us in the stone. "He had to learn, learn what the succubus' heart contained. Learn what his own heart contained and how it would answer," it cackled, then smiled and disappeared.

I groaned, reaching up to touch the goose egg forming on my skull.

"Hey, is that offer to carry me still good?"

He raised an eyebrow at that. Neither of us wanted to dive into what The Oracle had said. I didn't have a heart, after all.

"I don't remember offering to carry you." The corner of his lip twitched.

"Really? I swear I heard that offer." Groaning, I rolled to my side, still beneath him. "You planning on moving, big boy?"

Logan smiled in earnest. "Do you want to talk about what The Oracle said, about our hearts?"

I squinted up at him, finding my vision a little blurry.

"Nope."

With a huff, he pulled me up jerkily.

"Is it me or is our platform moving?" I asked, hanging my head over the edge, trusting Logan to keep hold of me.

"We are moving."

"Great, the express. I'll be sure to negotiate that in future trips," I slurred.

"What makes you think there will be future trips?"

Heaving my shoulders up to pull back my head took more effort than I expected. We came to an abrupt stop that had me leaning into Logan's warm body.

Shaking my head, I stepped down, only to misjudge the distance and land on my ass, again.

Logan hauled me up and slung me over his shoulder. If I wasn't so busy trying to get the ground to stop spinning and my stomach under control I would have protested; as it was, I didn't mind. That fact right there should explain how far out of my mind I really was.

"Keys?" he questioned, his large hands roaming over my ass, trying to dig into my back pockets.

"Find them?" I asked, exhaustion weighing heavily on me.

"Do not fall asleep."

"No guarantees."

"What? Hell, you are going to see Gunner."

"Gunther? I don't need my hair and makeup done."

"No, Gunner. The guy the vamps kidnapped back on the Puppet Master case? Remember, he stitched you up a few times. He was the one who figured out what all the kids had in common."

"Oh, Gunner. I'm fine, I don't need to see—"

Darkness stole the rest of that sentence. What felt like days later, I regained consciousness, again slung over Logan's shoulder as he took the metal ladder down into Gunner's domain.

"Ugh," I grunted, pressing my hands into the small of Logan's back. I squinted in the bright lights, trying to get my bearings.

I sure as shit didn't expect Blake and Angelina to be staring back at me.

"Fucking hell. I think I'm hallucinating."

"Why, what are you seeing?" Gunner asked, pushing his glasses back up his nose.

"Heartbreaking, favor-sucking, asshole vampires."

Gunner blinked his large eyes at me a few times, digesting that, before Logan turned me around so I was facing the ladder.

"Blake and Angelina are here, Olie."

"Fucking hell, I'm leaving."

"The hell you are," Logan scolded, tightening his grip on my legs.

"Bring her in here," Gunner said, moving through the tables littered with miscellaneous electronic parts and back to a fluorescent metal room that stung my eyes.

Logan lowered me down softly to sit on the table. Gunner closed the door behind him.

"I hate them," I whined to Logan.

Gently, he stroked the side of my face. "I know."

"Why are you being so nice to me?" My filter had totally left.

"I'm not, you are hallucinating." He crossed his arms over his chest, removing the soft touch I was finding comfort in.

I squinted at him, swaying slightly, but before I could form a suitable comeback the door creaked open, revealing a dark haired soul crusher.

I couldn't help the groan.

"I just have one question," Blake said softly, his brilliant cobalt eyes latching onto me and threatening to crush the small parts of my dignity I had left.

"What are you doing here?" I hissed. "Vampires don't need help to heal."

Blake shifted his stance, his eyes becoming guarded. "We needed blood." He shook his head sadly. "Angelina tried to storm the House holding my niece."

"Fucking bitch," I muttered, shocked, followed by "bullshit."

The door swung open farther, revealing the bitch in question. "My doings are none of your concern."

"Oh fucking hell," I yelled unsteadily, slipping from the table. "You know that is of my concern, and you know you didn't actually expect to get her, especially with your Master in town. A failed attempt at acquiring her would undoubtedly land you in some sort of sordid punishment, which you would probably enjoy. Furthermore, you are only trying to endear yourself to Blake, although why is beyond me since you already mated the soul-sucking asshole.

Unless of course, he and Tate are unhappy with your false promises of obtaining their family member."

Her eyes narrowed at my tirade. Thankfully, I still had enough undamaged brain cells not to disclose that Angelina had redeemed the favor I owed Blake. Ugh, actually...

"What did you want to ask me?" I groaned, leaning heavily against the table again.

"What did you mean by 'favor-sucking?'"

Exhaling forcefully, I looked at Angelina. "It's a little known fact that once a couple is mated—as in forever and ever, only death can separate us—any and all favors owed to one party easily transfer to the other."

Slowly, Blake looked down at Angelina. "Did you call in my favor with Olivia?"

Her eyes bored into me, but I was too unstable to give a fuck.

"Blake, this really isn't the time," the bitch tried, laying a soothing hand on his arm. He jerked away from her touch.

"Answer the question, mate." The last word was hissed with equal measures of disgust and rage.

Angelina dropped the poor, pathetic, injured me act, glaring back at Blake. I slipped against the table and into the welcome warmth of Logan, whose hands rested gently, but firmly, on my hips.

Angelina caught the movement, her lips smirking. "And what happened to you tonight? Demon whore got it good?"

I lifted a hand to reject her comment before I remembered Bear. "Not tonight, but yeah, I did." I watched Blake's eyes flash amber with anger at the comment, before he remembered and looked away from me. His intense gaze focused on Logan for a moment and I smiled.

"Wrong shifter," I informed, him gloating.

Gunner moved past the pissed off vampires into the room. "What happened, Olie?" he asked, gently probing my head. Logan helped me sit back down on the exam table.

"She fell from a sheer rock face onto more rock, after we rock climbed without harnesses," Logan answered.

Gunner looked between us. "The Oracle?" he asked.

Angelina hissed, "You know where she is?"

I smiled, a lopsided, slightly dazed smile. "Bet you wish you had traded his favor for that information."

She pushed into the room eagerly. "I'll make it easier for you, take me to The Oracle and I won't make you—" She stopped, looking back at Blake, realizing her slip.

Anger flared his nostrils, an unneeded breath hissing though his lips. "You lying bitch. That was your plan all along, to have Olivia do your dirty work with a favor she owed me."

My heart softened towards him, my Blake. He had been mine for such a brief moment, and in that time wrecked my entire heart. Destroyed my carefully constructed walls and broken through where others had failed. I missed him terribly.

He took an involuntary step towards me. "Olie," he whispered, the regret, the knowledge of his mistake evident in his eyes.

I felt my tears plopping onto my lap. "It's too late," I whispered. He reached out to cradle my face and I pulled back, unable to look at him. "You made your decision, Blake." I forced myself to face him. "I truly doubt I will ever be able to love another after you, but I know I deserve more than this," I said, waving my hand to indicate the Angelina drama. Sucking down a breath, I continued, "I'll rescue your niece, though, have no doubt. I pay my debts."

With that, I turned to Gunner and let him administer his much-needed treatments. I didn't hear them leave but I knew when they did, based on Logan's body relaxing.

"S-Sorry," Gunner stuttered. "I didn't mean to cause problems."

I looked at the open door, my grief changing into something I didn't yet understand. "It was perfect, Gunner. The truth will set us free."

Chapter 16

After Gunner had done his best with me, including a magic potion he purchased from a witch—serious doubts there—Logan and I made our way to his storage unit. We needed additional accessories for our upcoming battle with the wicked witches.

"Why do you store the good shit away from your home?"

Logan shrugged, slipping out of the vehicle as I moved around to hear his response. "When I first got here, there wasn't a guarantee I would be staying." He moved easily, muscle rippling under his replacement shirt as he rolled up the storage door.

"Why are you staying, anyways?"

Logan shrugged again, pulling a long black duffel bag onto a metal table in the middle of the room.

"Closer to family?" I taunted in a singsong voice.

He shrugged for a third time. Sliding up on the table, I didn't let up. "Coming around to your senses about the hussy?"

He raised one honey colored eyebrow at me, daring me to continue. I took the bait. "Maybe you just love the excitement of being close to the Supernatural Council."

"And by excitement you mean death and the constant threat thereof?"

I laughed. "As I recall, you brought the Puppet Master to my door."

"Not one of my finest moments," he reluctantly admitted.

"No, no, it certainly is a long line of mistakes made by our Alpha," an unknown voice stated behind us.

Logan stilled in his loading, as I turned to see who was going to start shit now.

A short, silver haired idiot sauntered into Logan's storage room. His swagger was cocky, though he had only a fraction of the muscle Logan's body boasted of. Deep wrinkles lined his face. He must have been ancient to actually get wrinkles.

"And you are going to do something about it?" Me and my mouth.

His smug look should have concerned me, but we had just escaped death. I had told Blake no, and we were surrounded by weapons. I was feeling mighty confident.

When the other four fell in behind him, it occurred to me I really should have seen that coming.

"You take these two, I'll take the rest," my cocky ass informed Logan.

"Pfft, please, I'll let you have one."

"One? Geez, now that's just insulting."

He turned his gaze toward me. "It was supposed to be protective."

"In a demeaning, I-can't-fight-since-I'm-a-girl way."

"Can't say I thought it through that far."

"If you two idiots are finished, I'll be killing you now," Silver Hair said.

"Who are you, anyways?" I questioned, annoyed our conversation was interrupted.

"Eli, and I'll be taking over now. I've been patiently waiting, gathering power and supporters in order to rectify the grievous errors Logan has led us into as Alpha." He stood perfectly straight. "It's time for the wolves to be in their proper position of power."

"I get him, Olie. I want to know how he was able to disguise his scent and approach."

"Fine," I grumbled, seeing the logic of Logan having to deal with the main threat. "So, are we going to do this, or is there official 'I challenge the Alpha' language?" I asked, deepening my voice.

Logan and Eli both gave me disbelieving looks like, "What? That's what the romance novels say."

With a huff Logan tore his shirt. "Show off," I muttered.

He shrugged. "It was bound to be ruined anyways, hanging out with you."

A growl had me turning my attention as the dark silver wolf of Eli launched at Logan. That was the fastest shift I had ever seen. Eli's extended claws scored the naked flesh of Logan, opening four fresh lines of blood across his chest.

"Humpf," I grunted, as I was suddenly slammed to the cold concrete on my side, landing heavily on my right wrist and shoulder.

Good news, they were in human form, with human arms wrapped around my middle. Bad news, I couldn't reach my dagger hidden in the small of my back. With a grunt I rolled to my other side, pinning the asshole under me, wiggling my arms.

"Hold her!" another flunkie yelled, holding out zip ties.

"Oh hell to the fuck no," I whispered, wrenching my top arm free in a fit of both desperation and annoyance at my inattention. Clenching my fist, I cracked it into his exposed neck, shutting down his windpipe.

"Heal from that, fucker."

Launching to my feet, I pulled the dagger at my back. "Let's fucking dance," I invited the other three. While they were highly unintelligent to attack us, I'd have to give them a few points in the not-a-complete-waste-of-space column for looking properly terrified.

I'm pretty sure I grinned at that fact.

"Call the zombies!" one of them screamed, backing up.

I paid no attention to the growling next to me as Logan and Eli slammed into a rack of guns together.

"What zombies?" I asked, stepping outside of the storage unit. The three remaining shifters were moving back behind a row of zombies, two deep.

"Where is a necromancer when you need one?" I sighed. How the fuck was this even possible?

Slowly, they lumbered toward me. Not in the mood to wait, I ran at them, slicing across putrid flesh, my stomach cramping from the vile smells. Spinning around, I caught an arm with loose flesh that was ready to slam down on my already healing head. Ducking down, I buried my blade into the loose muscle in his thigh, pulling forcefully and removing the limb from his body.

I can't say it was my most well thought-out plan, as the zombie fell on top of me while I struggled to clear off the dead flesh from my blade. With a grunt and a poorly executed roll, I dislodged the fallen zombie and cleaned off my blade.

I couldn't tell you what made me look up, what made me check on Logan, but I did. While he was busy fending off Eli, who was trying to take bites out of Logan's now furry hide, the asshole flunky was creeping steadily toward him in wolf form, belly low to the ground.

Not on my watch fucker, you want to take out the leader of the Shifter Nation you go through me.

"Logan, behind you!"

The shift in my attention earned me a zombie latching on to my forearm, but thankfully, not my throwing arm. I pulled out the blade at my back, balancing it by the tip before launching it with force.

Logan turned, meeting my eyes for a split second before the zombie horde I had been keeping at bay launched themselves with renewed force. I lost sight of him as I fell beneath a pile of rotting flesh.

Dammit.

Flat on my back, I struggled to keep my mouth closed as half decayed teeth chomped down on my appendages. It was bad enough that the smell would destroy this outfit. I was not going to swallow anything these fuckers were throwing out.

One of them bit through my leather pants and into the tender flesh of my thigh. I forgot myself, letting loose an open-mouthed scream.

I could hear the sounds of Logan fighting with the wolf, even above the chomping of the zombies on my body. Rolling onto my side, I crushed the jaw of the zombie on my thigh, embedding the flat teeth even deeper into my already tender flesh. My legs free, I began kicking my way out from the walking dead.

With a final heave, I stood, brushing bits of undead flesh from my jacket.

Logan nodded, acknowledging I was still breathing, before renewing his attack on the wolf.

As I reached down to remove the jaw from my thigh, I saw movement from the corner of my eye, too fast to be a zombie. My breath left me as I was tackled to the ground by another wolf. His attack sent us skidding across the floor back into the storage room, and again I lost sight of Logan, preoccupied as I was with my own shifter issues.

The wolf rolled off me, baring his teeth with menace as he crouched to launch at my jugular.

I'd had enough. Pulling a gun from the racks behind me, I took a gamble it was loaded and squeezed the trigger four times. The shifter dropped midair, landing at my feet and trying to pull himself away to heal.

"Fuck you," I told him before emptying my clip of, thank the Gods, bullets into his head. I suppose the gun might appear a strange item for Logan to stock, but being powerful always means having enemies, both within one's species and outside.

"I am done with this shit!" I screamed, marching back to where I'd last seen Logan.

What I saw there dumbfounded me. Logan had Eli, the silver shifter, pinned to the ground, Logan's massive jaws clenching down on the skull of the wolf.

Lorraine was on her knees, sobbing. "Let him go, please Logan," she whispered, hands clutched in front of her.

Hearing my footsteps, they all turned to me.

"Kill him," was my vote.

Logan growled, tightening his jaw. I smiled upon hearing the bones crack and pop.

"I'M PREGNANT!" Lorraine screamed.

Shock alone had Logan opening his mouth, but then I saw his eyes growing hopeful. The silver wolf was no fool, seizing the opportunity to beat a hasty retreat while Logan's gaze was locked on Lorraine.

"Aww shit Logan, REALLY? You don't even know if it is yours! What the fuck are you doing here anyway, Lorraine?"

Logan's eyes narrowed again as he sniffed Lorraine, completely ignoring me. Shifters could smell pregnancy. Kass had told me how Darren had been the one to sit her down and tell her she was knocked up. I was hoping she was lying, really, really fucking hoping. But when Logan's lion gently rubbed his head against her stomach I knew it was, at least, a partial truth from her.

I refused to acknowledge the disappointment or the trickle of loss that wanted to flood my emotions. Nor was I thinking about what The Oracle had said, or my curiosity about what might have blossomed between us. Nope, wasn't thinking about any of it.

Logan shifted back to human form and I took myself out of the storage unit. I didn't need to hear any of this, nor did I need the temptation of looking below his nonexistent belt.

"When?" Logan whispered, dammit for still being able to hear. I moved around the SUV and slid down, staring at the bite marks on my legs.

"Only a few days ago," her shaky voice answered. "I was avoiding you, until I knew for certain."

"Is it mine?" Logan asked, with heartbreaking hope in his voice.

"Of course," the hussy lied.

"Why are you here?" Steel coated Logan's words. I was glad to see the pregnancy announcement hadn't totally deluded him.

"I was coming to check on you." More lies.

"Bullshit Lorraine, you were one of two people I told I was coming here and the other was my brother."

"I've always said he was untrustworthy."

"Why, Lorraine?" Logan's voice was soft either from anger or hurt, I wasn't sure.

"Does it matter?" She sounded tired.

"Yes." Logan's answer was clipped.

"You replaced me with her!" she screamed, stomping her foot. "The place beside you was for me and you let her have it."

Silence descended.

"Who is Eli to you?" His voice was deadly quiet.

"I've been seeing him for a few months. He promised I would be his Queen."

"Want me to slap her?" I hollered.

"No, she's pregnant. But I would appreciate your help with her."

I was not feeling excited about his wanting my help. Not. At. All.

Dragging myself back to an upright position, I winced as I put weight on my thigh. Logan's gaze hadn't left Lorraine, nor had he put clothing on.

"Clothing, Logan," I reminded him. "I'll protect the now pregnant wannabe queen bitch."

His gaze cut swiftly to me. I rolled my eyes. "Nor will I hit her."

He gave me a curt nod before rummaging in one of the black plastic totes.

"Who is Eli?" I asked point blank, while shifting my weight to my uninjured leg.

Lorraine fiddled with the hem of her top, shrugging.

Now was usually the time when I would smack, hit, threaten or maim someone who had just betrayed me, but the pregnancy forced a change in my approach. Unfortunately, the little life inside of her hadn't done anything to deserve my brutality.

"Don't play games, Lorraine, we know you set us up based on your timely appearance. And we now know Eli holds a very special place in your heart for you to BEG for his life."

She didn't glance at me, instead trying to hold Logan's gaze as he arrived back next to me, standing closer to me than her.

Lorraine pulled out a winning smile, reaching out to touch Logan. He recoiled, his gaze riveted to her, her fingers brushing empty air.

"Answer her question."

"Logan, don't do this, please."

"Betrayal is not something I am capable of forgiving." Thank the Gods. "Answer Olivia."

"Or what?" Lorraine taunted, crossing her arms. "I can abort the pregnancy."

Logan stepped forward then, anger rippling along his arms, "You'd kill your own child for spite?"

"I can disappear, you will never see us again."

"Switching tactics won't help you, Lorraine," I warned. "From this moment you will be accompanied by someone loyal to Logan or myself twenty four hours a day. You will not be allowed to grocery shop, shower, or even shit alone while you are carrying Logan's child. We protect our own, and we protect it ruthlessly."

I hadn't realized I had stepped forward until I pulled back.

"I have rights," she hissed, her chin trembling.

I smiled. "Not if you disappear."

She turned to Logan again, properly terrified, although why I have no idea. I had just told her she would be protected to the highest degree and that scared her. I had to be missing something.

"You wouldn't cage me up, Logan. You trust me."

I couldn't help the scoff that left my lips as I turned my attention to him.

"You can arrange that?" he asked me softly.

"Of course," I answered quickly. "She has to be protected, even if it is from herself."

His warm hand rested on my shoulder with approval as he spoke. "It doesn't matter who he was to you, Lorraine. I will find him and I will kill him. You will be protected from harming yourself and the child. Do not think that others will not attempt to kill you as well. You are carrying my child, a powerful child."

Lifting her chin, she attempted to appear brave.

"How does Eli have access to zombies?" Logan asked.

She shook her head. If she did know, she wasn't spilling.

I turned to Logan. "It doesn't matter. We will figure it out."

He nodded, turning his attention back to Lorraine. With a pent-up breath I dictated, "Let's get our gear, call a cleanup crew, and regroup at my security compound."

"The manor would be better," Logan grunted, filling a duffel bag with all sorts of pretties.

"I'm not taking her around the children."

"I'm more stable than you are around the children," Lorraine declared, her head held high. It sure didn't take her long to go back to being a stuck-up bitch.

"Can you get her into the SUV?" Logan asked, two full duffel bags hanging from his shoulders. Thank goodness I couldn't see the outline of his bulging biceps or the strength in his shoulders. Ugh, damn him and his skintight undershirt.

"Yeah, I got it." Turning to Lorraine I asked, "You going to walk, or do I have to carry you?"

"I can walk." Crossing her arms over her chest, she proved she still had the ability to move one foot in front of another, getting into the back seat. I made quick work of enabling the childproof locks; I wasn't about to put anything past this bitch.

Logan pulled me back to his storage room, picking me up and setting me on the table.

I raised an eyebrow. "What are you doing?"

"Your leg needs to be cleaned."

I looked down at the wound on my leg. "Probably," I agreed.

"Leathers off or you want me to cut them?"

I sighed, debating. "Just cut them, like you said they are already ruined from our adventures."

Rubbing the back of my neck, I watched Logan work. He carefully pulled the fabric away from the scarlet wound, oozing puss. "Fucking zombies," I hissed as Logan pushed on the wound, sending additional puss shooting out.

"It's already infected."

"Of course it is. Did you see how decrepit those assholes were?"

I paused at that statement. "They must be from the cemetery, but why didn't they attack with all the other zombies, and how did a rogue shifter get a hold of them?"

"I don't know. Hold still, this is going to hurt."

"OWW!" I wiggled on the table, clenching my hands around a metal lip that cut into my fingers. Logan put a warm, strong hand on my hip, holding me still as he cleaned.

...

Finally, with my wounds cleaned, I hoisted myself into the SUV and called Becky while Logan piled the goodies into the back.

"Boss," she answered.

"I have a new project for you." I hated that she called me that, but I was having a hard time recalling why.

She grunted a reply.

"I need you to find a man named Eli, silver haired, wolf shifter, trying to kill Logan."

She laughed, "You need to notify next of kin?"

I cut a glance to Logan buckling up in the passenger seat. "We will," he confirmed.

"Oh hey there, Kitty, didn't know you were with boss lady."

I clamped a hand against my mouth, trying to fight the giggles. Logan leaned forward toward the center console. "Kitty?" he repeated in disbelief.

I could hear Becky's gum chomping. "That's what the boss calls you."

He turned to me, shocked. "You call me Kitty?"

I smiled. "There are so many bad jokes to be had right now, but we're up against the clock. Beck, I need you to find a pair of executioners who can stay in town for the next ten months."

Clicking met my request. "Hmm, Blue asked for some time off, and I bet I could get Victoria on the assignment if Blue is around."

"Do it. We will be there shortly."

"Can do, Boss." She hung up on me with a preoccupied click.

"Kitty?" Logan repeated, a smile tugging at his lips.

"I fail to see the problem."

"Only one issue at a time, and we currently have two on our plate."

Three if we tossed in Blake and Angelina, but who was counting?

...

Becky had printed out what she found on Eli and it wasn't pretty. Logan skimmed the file after I was done with it. He gave a low whistle.

"Did you know your boyfriend has a history of mental illness?" Logan asked Lorraine.

"He said you would say that, you would try to discredit the true hero he is."

"Let's add expert manipulator to his list of things to keep the fuck away from," I muttered.

Becky nodded, her fingers flying over the keyboard. "Not sure it would take an expert, though," she added. Brutally honest, one of the many features I like about her.

I laughed, wincing at the throbbing it caused, rubbing the back of my head.

"You need to sleep, boss," Becky informed me.

I groaned, "I look that bad?"

"Yep."

I patted her back. "You got a plush holding cell for Lorraine?"

"Yep, complete with fresh towels."

"Perfect," Logan growled.

...

We took the file back to Logan's place and had it spread out between us on his bed, working until the words blurred and my stomach clenched from lack of sleep.

"Take my bed. I can't sleep there tonight," Logan told me, standing and stretching hard-packed muscles.

I lay back. "Ugh, can you look at my leg? It isn't throbbing, but better safe than sorry."

"Sure."

He leaned over, crumpling the paperwork as he peeled back his carefully applied bandages. "You'll last for a few more hours."

I grunted a response, already slipping off to sleep.

"Night, Olie."

...

My phone was vibrating in my pocket, and while I knew I should answer it, I just couldn't bring myself to do it.

Logan's phone rang next and he groaned before answering it. Squinting my dry eyes at him, I jerked when he sprang from the bed.

"What hospital? ... Okay, we're on our way." Wasn't he supposed to be in a guest bed somewhere?

"Yeah," he said, turning to look at me. "Olie is here."

Shoving myself into a sitting position, I cringed at the tightness in my thigh. The zombie wound was still healing. As I swung my legs down I rubbed at the back of my neck, knotted up from the awkward position I had slept in.

"Let's go. Kass is having the baby."

Rubbing my eyes, I looked over at him. "Logan, we need to shower the dried blood and zombie gunk off."

He nodded, his hands fiddling with the phone. "Yeah, you're probably right."

I stood and moved around the bed, shoving him towards the shower. "Go. I have to grab my bag from the SUV."

He nodded absentmindedly, chucking his clothing on his walk to the bathroom. I averted my eyes from the golden, firm-skinned man. Sleeping with Logan would complicate everything. Not that he wanted to, although he had been nicer lately.

I shook my head, letting myself out the front door and pulling open the back door of my SUV to get the trusty military surplus duffel bag there, hoisting it over my shoulder. At least my head felt better.

Instead of showering in Logan's room—why I had decided to review the files in his room was also beyond me—I opted for the guest room on the first floor. Pushing open the door, I tried not to dwell on memories of what had transpired between Blake and me. It felt like a lifetime ago that I was helping manage Mark's pain in a hospital and having healing sex with Blake to recover.

Now I was going to a hospital for a different reason, a better reason, but I probably wasn't as excited as I should be. Kass giving birth to a child only made my own lack of fertility weigh heavier on me. I was jealous of my friend and I shouldn't be. I should be happy.

I should have been a lot of things that I wasn't. I was just a broken succubus with an unhinged need to kill.

...

Logan was waiting for me in the front room, freshly showered in navy blue jeans that highlighted his firm thighs, paired with a gray shirt hugging those pecs and biceps. I was not looking, at all, not even a peek. Yeah, I'm not buying it either.

In my own jeans and royal blue t-shirt, I watched him busily texting.

"Ready?" I asked, slinging my bag over my shoulder.

He grunted what I assumed was an affirmative. I listened to him lock up and set his alarm as I loaded my bag back into my SUV.

Kass was having the baby. Excitement was beginning to wedge its annoying way through my exhaustion and worry. Checking my industrial watch, I saw we had lost eight hours between dealing with Lorraine and sleeping.

"I'll drive," Logan demanded, snagging the keys out of my back pocket hurriedly.

"She's only in labor, it can take hours." He wasn't listening. "I'm not even sure why we are going."

Logan stomped on the gas, skidding out of his driveway. "Because we have been asked to. It's called support."

...

Logan steered us within the hospital much the same way he had in the car, recklessly pushing forward. I followed along through long hallways, the sterile walls occasionally interrupted by drab artwork.

As we waited to get buzzed through the locked doors, a small voice screamed my name.

"Hannah," I whispered, turning around and running. I recognized the tendrils of pain, fear, and loneliness in her call, but more than that, as I rounded a corner, I could feel it.

Lee and Jane were in the hallway with her as she screamed my name again, fists tightly balled at her sides, eyes closed, head tipped back. The hallway was crowded. At the busy nurses' station all eyes were trained on her breakdown. More importantly, she was influencing those around her, pushing her own tiny but intense emotions into those nearby.

"Hannah!" I yelled, still running at her.

Lee and Jane turned, their faces tear-stained, eyes wild, inner beasts slamming against their tight control. Dropping down on a knee, I slid between them, wrapping my arms around Hannah and throwing up shields around us.

153

"Easy, baby girl, I'm here."

"Olie, they won't let me see Kass, and Daddy went in the room with her. What if she dies like my mommy?" Her small voice cracked, tears spilling down her face.

Her emotions slammed into my barriers. I focused on calming my breathing and holding her delicate body in my arms, her head snuggled into my neck. Logan touched my back before also placing a hand on Hannah's.

I was impressed that he could stand the emotional assault. Then again, he had also been unafraid to touch me when I was pumping Morgan full of anger.

This close, he could surely feel the emotion she was pushing out, yet he didn't seem bothered.

"Hey peanut," he said, gently stroking her back.

"Uncle Logan, I'm scared." Her voice was soft in my ear as I tightened my arms around her and swayed.

Logan squatted down and wrapped his arms around both of us, dropping a kiss against Hannah's hair.

I wanted to promise her everything would be okay, that I wouldn't allow anything to happen to Kass, but those were promises I couldn't make.

The future is promised to no one.

I kept pushing out tranquility and peacefulness to Hannah and the surrounding area. Slowly, the tension dimmed and the probing eyes relented.

"Hannah, sweetie, can you control your emotions now?" I asked gently as she pulled back to look at me. Logan was a warm safety blanket, his distracting chest pushing against us.

Slowly, she nodded. "Sorry."

"Its okay, sweetheart," Logan comforted her, stroking her hair.

"Uncle Logan and Olivia, you go fix Kass NOW!"

"Okay sweetie," Logan agreed, taking her from me before going over to his parents.

Jane wiped her brow of sweat. "So you deal with that all the time?"

I smiled, tucking a lock of hair behind Hannah's ear. "We struggle with our emotions constantly, to not influence those around us. It's a never ending battle."

Logan handed Hannah to Lee. "Glad you showed up when you did," Lee said, nodding his approval. "But I do think Kass needs you. She has been in labor for ten hours."

"Ten hours!" Logan bellowed.

My hand shot out a warning, prickling against his skin.

"I mean, only ten hours? I guess we might go peak our heads in," he amended.

I smirked, kissing Hannah. "I'll be back, sweet pea. Can you go find me something to eat?"

She nodded and hung her head over Lee's shoulder. I may not be able to have children, but I would always enjoy them.

Blowing out a breath, Logan and I turned to go back down the hallway. Our steps echoed on the industrial laminate, my fists clenching and releasing at my sides without my conscious knowledge.

Logan picked up the tan phone in front of the locked maternity ward. "We are here to see Kass Moore.

"...Yes, I am aware she is in labor ... Kass requested Olivia ... Yes, she is with me ... We are a package deal."

The door finally buzzed as I peered at him with a raised eyebrow. "Apparently, only you are allowed to pass," he intoned with sarcastic solemnity.

"Come on, you overgrown kitty," I teased, pulling him along behind me. "Do you know what room?"

"Three sixteen."

Skirting the nurses' station, I landed a soft knock. "Kass?" I called out tentatively.

"GET YOUR ASS IN HERE!" came the screaming reply.

As we slipped into the room, Logan pulled on my hand. "Can Logan come in?" I called, before breaching the flimsy privacy curtain.

Darren slipped around the peach fabric, his face pale and haggard. "Let's get food," he said, pulling Logan behind him.

He and Logan made their way down the hallway, Logan sending me an uncertain gaze. I tried giving him a reassuring smile, but based on his frown, I wasn't succeeding.

Passing the curtain, I plastered on a smile for the sweat-soaked Kass. She lay curled on her side, tears leaking down her face.

"Hey sweetie," I began, softening my voice.

"This is terrible," she hissed, not turning toward me.

Resting my hand on her forearm, I slowly trickled out peacefulness.

"I got pain meds, they're helping. Darren leave?"

"He went to get food with Logan."

"Figures, I can't even eat, I throw everything up." Rolling over slowly to look at me, she whispered, "I'm scared."

"Of what?"

"Of the pain, of taking care of a little baby. What if I'm terrible at it? My own mother left me." Her drawn brows pulled lower, fear and worry pulsing from her body.

"That is exactly the reason you will excel at being a mom. Look at Hannah, she already adores you." I gave her a small smile.

"I had to send her out," she whimpered. "I couldn't let her see me like this."

"That's okay."

"Hi Kass, it's time to check on the baby's heartbeat," a chipper brown-haired nurse announced, laying a monitor low on Kass' swollen stomach.

"Are you getting any rest?" she asked, watching the numbers intently.

"A little."

"Heartbeat looks great, do you need anything?"

Kass shook her head and the nurse made her way out.

A new emotion pricked at my awareness, a deep set contentment. Tilting my head, I looked down at Kass' belly.

"Do you feel that?" she asked in a hushed whisper.

I couldn't help the grin stretching my lips. "I do."

"Oh GOD! Get Darren! He is coming!"

Thankfully, Darren must have been close by. He burst into the room, flinging the peach curtain aside and clasping Kass's other hand.

"Logan's getting the nurse, sweetie," Darren comforted, stroking her forehead.

"Easy, Darren," I whispered. "Calm down, the baby can feel you."

His startled gaze and open mouth had a million questions, but he was stalled when Kass cried out again.

"Focus on your breathing, Kass," he soothed.

The new awareness was readying, strengthened by Darren's presence. I kept the calm energy flowing through my fingers to Kass. Her breathing, while labored, evened out.

The nurse came back, shifting Kass to her back and checking her.

"Great news, it's almost time to push. I'll get the doctor."

...

Three hours later, I was holding Harrison in my arms, swaying and humming to him while Kass and Darren slept.

"You have to share him," Logan reminded me, drumming his hands on his thighs. He made the hospital chairs look dainty.

"Pfft, nope."

Hannah had been relieved and exhausted once Kass and her new brother were safe; her grandparents had carted her home for some much needed sleep. I gave them the manor's number and told them to call if Hannah struggled with her emotions again.

Pressing a light kiss against his swaddled hand, I passed the tiny bundle to Logan, who looked both awkward and handsome holding the small tyke.

"We still have to get Jerry," Logan reminded me.

"We will," I agreed, calmed by Harrison's arrival and strengthening resolve. I checked my almost indestructible watch. "We have time."

Harrison gave a squawk, one little fist reaching out of his swaddle. "He's strong," Logan breathed, as he smiled down at his nephew.

"He is loved," I answered, enjoying the quiet moment.

...

Logan carefully lowered the sleeping Harrison into the bassinet next to the sleeping parents, briefly resting his enormous hand on the baby's small body.

His lip ticked up a small smirk, probably envisioning his own little tyke being grown in the belly of the wannabe queen bitch. At least one good thing would come out of it. I was officially off the hook for planning their wedding. Thank you, cheating bitch. Although I'm not sure we had decided the child was Logan's, we had certainly made assumptions to that effect.

Quietly leaving the room behind us, we spent the walk to the car in silent retrospection.

"You driving?" Logan asked.

I chewed my thumbnail, squinting in the settling daylight, finally shaking my head. "Let's go to the manor. Tommy should be home and I need his help to pinpoint where The Oracle showed me."

He grunted and we slid into the SUV together.

"So she didn't show you an address?"

"It doesn't work that way. She showed me the location of where we can find Jerry and when, but it wasn't an address, just an intersection."

"Which was?"

"Main and Becker."

"Why don't we find it and go now?"

I sighed. "The Oracle is not a transparent help. It's best to adhere to the time and place she shows."

He drummed his fingers on the steering wheel. "I don't like it."

Releasing a breath, I leaned my head against the headrest, looking up at the visor in front of me. "I agree, but we have to get Jerry back, nothing else matters." Mark's desolate eyes haunted me.

"If I can only do one thing right, it will be this," I added with my jaw set hard.

"Why does it only have to be one thing? You've lived this long."

I gave a short, humorless laugh. "Twenty-four years, such an accomplishment."

Logan cut a shocked glance my way. "You are twenty-four?"

"Yeah, how old did you think I was?"

"Not twenty-four. Older, much older."

I smiled, toying with a violet strand of hair. "I'll be lucky to see thirty."

Logan shifted in the seat. "Don't be foolish."

"I'm not. I'm realistic and a planner."

Logan pulled into the manor after security cleared us. I was done with this conversation and I was done feeling sorry for myself. Silence descended as we stomped up the stairs to Tommy's room; rather, I stomped up the stairs. Heads peeked out of rooms and quickly ducked back in. At Tommy's door, I knocked on a poster of some strange anime character.

"Yo Olie!" Tommy yelled though the door. "You may enter."

Pushing open the door I asked, "How did you know it was me?"

158

"Security cameras. I monitor the feed with Becky." He remained fixated on the screens in front of him, his back to us.

I smiled and nodded as I ruffled his dark locks, leaning to look over his shoulder.

"I need you to find an intersection, Main and Becker."

Logan leaned against the desk that hardly contained Tommy's three monitors, each one quickly flashing information that I couldn't track.

"Do you have any more details? Like the state?" Tommy asked, looking up at me in disbelief.

"No," I grunted, hovering over his shoulder. "I'll know it when I see it, though."

"Want to explain how that works?"

Leaning my arm on the back of his chair, I propped my chin on my hand. "So, I went to see The Oracle—"

"Wait, THE Oracle?" Tommy asked me, turning to face me and throwing me off my resting spot.

"Yeah, unless there is another one I don't know of."

"Wow." Tommy spun back in his chair and I took that as an invitation to continue.

"And she told me I could find Jerry on Main and Becker in about a day and a half."

"Humph."

"Then The Oracle tried to kill her," Logan felt the need to add.

"WHAT?" Tommy squeaked, turning again to face me.

I shrugged a shoulder, staring daggers at Logan before turning to assure Tommy, "She tried, but she failed."

"Did you kill her?" he asked in awe.

"No, the bitch is badder than me."

Logan stifled a laugh, asking, "How hard was it for you to admit that?"

"Not at all," I lied, adjusting my shirt forcefully to hide my irritation.

I apparently did a poor job, as both Logan and Tommy were smirking. Asshole and asshole-in-training.

"What do you got for me?"

"You need pictures, I'm assuming."

"That would be ideal," I confirmed.

Tommy grunted, fingers again flying over the keyboard.

"Did you see Harrison?" Tommy asked.

"I did, he's adorable."

"He's a boy," Logan and Tommy informed me in unison.

I shrugged. "Still adorable."

"Alright, Olie, let's put The Oracle's information to the test. Assuming the intersection is within your boundaries, we can eliminate at least half, leaving eight intersections that match. Can you tell me anything else?"

I thought back to the memory. "The street signs are blue with white lettering."

"Okay, that takes care of another three." Tommy pulled up pictures of the remaining five intersections.

"That one." I pointed to a bustling downtown photo. Humans were everywhere in the revived industrial buildings, sipping on coffee, shopping, talking and laughing. Not good. Why couldn't they stay with their long tradition of abandoned industrial buildings?

Tommy let a low whistle out. "That's Nashville. They are having some huge music convention there in a day or so."

"Why would the witches open a portal to the Fae with a huge human audience?" Logan questioned.

"Sacrifices; blood magic to boost their power," I answered, running my index finger over my bottom lip, thinking. "What shops are on those corners?"

Tommy pulled up another view of the corner. "Only two shops, the street dead ends into a hotel. On the south side of the road is a coffee joint, and on the north is an art gallery."

"Can you get pictures of the coffee shop?" I asked, leaning over his shoulder.

"Olie, I'm insulted," Tommy teased.

I rested a hand on his shoulder, smiling as images assaulted my eyes. Ignoring the smiling faces in the pictures, I focused on the background, the corrugated sheet metal used as paneling for the bottom of the walls, the red tables, the reclaimed wood counter top, and the concrete-floored storage room.

"There," I pointed, leaving a finger smudge on his pristine computer screen. "That's where he will be."

"Can you get me the name of the hotel?" Logan asked.

"For real, you people don't listen!" Tommy huffed, annoyed.

Logan smirked. "Sorry Tommy, you have us both impressed."

He huffed an answer.

"The Majestic Hotel. You thinking of setting up camp there?" Tommy asked, spinning around as both Logan and I took a step back, he to make a call, and I to watch him, wondering the same thing.

"Can't hurt to be close," Logan agreed, before speaking to the person on the phone.

"You leavin' again?" Tommy asked, the sullen teenager peeking out from behind the computer genius.

"I have to get Jerry."

He nodded, not looking at me. Squatting in front of him, I took his hands in mine, letting the love I felt for him seep into his dark skin. "I'll be back, and I promise to spend an entire day and night here until you can't stand the sight of me."

"Really?" he hesitantly asked, raising a dark brow at me.

"For realz," I teased.

He shook his head, already recovered from the temporary emotional vulnerability.

"Ready?" Logan asked.

I stood, resting a hand on Tommy's shoulder. "Be good, kid. I'll be back."

I chose to ignore the pointed look Logan gave me. It read all kinds of see-I-told-you-so, aren't-you-glad-I-caught-you-at-The-Oracle. Passing by him, I teased, "Whenever you are, Kitty," trouble in my eyes.

"You are not allowed to call me that in public," he sternly reprimanded me.

"That ruins all my fun," I pouted, descending the stairs next to him.

"OLIE!" Grams called behind me.

I turned. "Hey," I greeted her, as she made her way down to Logan and me.

"Next week I'm taking a weekend off to get away with Mercer. Can you watch the manor and Mindy?"

"Yeah, you know if I—" Logan elbowed me, cutting off my next sentence. Turning on him with a glare, I amended, "Yeah, no problem."

"Lovely," she stated, clipping back up the stairs in her designer heels and pastel pink skirt and cream blouse.

"The kids don't need to hear that," Logan cautioned as we began our downward descent again.

"Oh, and what are you, a fucking expert on children now?" I hissed back at him, my protective nature going into overdrive.

He shook his head, holding the oversized front door open for me. "No, but I saw the way you and Tommy interact."

I shrugged, not willing to get into it. Some memories really should stay buried, and the memory of finding Tommy was one of those.

...

Scrubbing a hand over my face, I looked over at Logan in the driver's seat.

"It's a four hour drive, we should probably get started," I hinted.

He smiled, knowing I wanted to get going now that I had the intel. "I thought we shouldn't jump the gun, for the sake of 'destiny' and The Oracle."

Crossing my arms, I raised a brow at him. "The hotel is not the location The Oracle showed me."

"Technicalities."

"Whatever. Hurry up, let's get your bag packed so we can get on the road. I should probably update Mark."

I toyed with my phone before using the touch screen to place the call.

Mark answered on the first ring, groggily, "Olivia?"

"Hey Mark, I found Jerry." No use in delaying my news. A sharp intake of air met my announcement.

"Where?" he rasped out.

"Nashville, TN. Logan and I are headed out now, do you want us to pick you up?" I ignored the pointed look Logan was throwing me.

"Yes," he breathed out, amidst a massive exhale.

"Okay, be ready in thirty." I ended the call, ready for Logan's unneeded input.

"You shouldn't be involving him in this. He's too emotional, emotions cloud judgment."

"He needs to do something, needs to feel like he is helping get Jerry back. While I agree his judgment is clouded, I trust him to get Jerry to safety so we can deal with the bitchy witches. "

"Witches certainly are fairly low on the supernatural totem pole," Logan commented.

"For good reason," I grunted. "When I first took over, they sucked up the biggest share of my time with their petty disagreements, coven boundary disputes, and other useless drama. It got to the point where I finally banned them from the Council. Their numbers were plentiful, more than adequate to protect their own. Not being able to do so was not a good enough reason for me to keep getting involved."

Logan grunted. "They weren't always so lowly. At one point they were highly revered for their knowledge."

"Oh, how the mighty have fallen—and how the fuck old are you, anyways?" I asked as we pulled into Logan's driveway.

"Didn't anyone ever tell you it's rude to ask someone's age?"

I laughed, following him out of the car. "So you're really old."

He huffed, straightening his shirt. "Old enough to know something," he smoothed, throwing me a wink.

I laughed again, following him into the house. "Did you just flirt with me?"

"No, I most certainly did not." He was in front of me so I couldn't see his face, but I had the distinct feeling he was joking. I couldn't help but choose not to deal with it.

"Hurry up, princess," I yelled as we cleared the door and he headed up the stairs. It seemed that both of us were in better spirits, finally having a target and something to do.

I headed to his kitchen for some snacks.

Logan found me with an open container of prepackaged cookie dough, using a spoon to eat it.

"Really?"

"What?" I asked around a mouthful. "I'm hungry."

He shook his head. "Let's get a move on."

...

Mark was waiting for us with a black duffel bag and bags under his eyes to match. As we came to a stop, he threw his bag in before grunting and sliding in himself.

"Lay down," Logan ordered him. "Sleep."

I turned around, watching Mark's jaw twitch with irritation, his wolf itching for a fight.

"It's a four hour drive," I said, "and we don't plan on stopping for more than gas. I'll wake you when we get there." Reaching an arm back, I laid my hand on Mark's fist resting on his knee, seeping tranquility into him. His eyes rolled back into his head as exhaustion took over and he slumped over his bag.

"Did you just make him sleep?" Logan asked.

"No, I gave him a little peace and the lack of sleep finally caught up to him."

Logan grunted, "You going to sleep also?"

"Doubtful."

...

After a three hour and forty-five minute trip with a single pit stop for snacks and gas, we pulled into The Majestic. I tried to keep my gaze away from the coffee shop, failing repeatedly. Hoisting my bags, one of clothing and another of weapons, I followed the boys inside.

"Fancy luggage, Logan," I commented on his rolling suitcase.

"Jealous?" he asked.

Even Mark, who walked next to me looking a little more rested, cracked a small smile. Having something to kill was helping us all.

The hotel was lavish. The floors were pristine, the pearl tiles inscribed with a carefully scripted black onyx M. Black leather chairs enclosed a small sitting area with matching black tables and white lamps.

Logan looked at home striding to the lobby desk, while Mark and I shifted with unease, knowing we must be standing out like sore thumbs. Logan took the keys from the lady behind the desk and Mark snickered, "Looks like we are sharing a room."

"Damn shifter hearing," I sighed. "As if I wasn't jealous enough of the claws and fangs."

"You're jealous of fangs?" Mark asked as we fell in line with Logan, making the short trip to the elevators.

"Totally, I'd love to smile at someone and have gleaming fangs to terrify them with."

"You aren't very intimidating," Logan commented.

"I know," I huffed. "I have to kill to get any respect."

"Tragic," Mark agreed sarcastically.

"So, you and Mark sharing a bed?" I asked Logan.

Not breaking stride as we moved out of the elevator he replied, "I thought we would share a bed and give Mark some space."

I huffed, couldn't fight with that logic.

"How much longer?" Mark asked, following Logan through the now open room door.

I looked at my watch, "A few more hours, enough time to eat and get some rest before we need to scout out the location. Although I won't be able to go in."

"Why?" Mark asked, setting his duffel bag on a bed. I thumped my own two down next to Logan's on the bed closest to the window.

"I don't want to screw with The Oracle's prediction. We need to get Jerry and I don't have time to make another trip to her."

Mark nodded soberly.

"I call dibs on the shower," I announced, grabbing my toiletry bag and staking my claim.

...

When my fingers were pruned and I had made a valiant attempt at using all the hot water in the hotel, I finally emerged, wrapped in a towel.

"I'm out," I announced, rummaging though my bag and seeing Mark deeply engrossed in the file Becky had given us.

"Any thoughts on that?" I asked as Logan made his way into the shower.

I changed quickly, throwing on underwear under the towel along with soft cloth shorts, and then displacing the towel by sliding on a tank top. Forget bras, I was done wearing one for a few hours.

"Like how the zombies managed to not only appear in Ohio but also in St. Ann," I continued, "with two different groups of people?"

"They are probably working together. Destiny gave him a few zombies so they could split up and take care of business, her opening a portal and him killing Logan."

"That's so obvious it hurts that I missed it."

He sent me an understanding smile. "Fresh eyes."

I groaned, pulling back the comforter and crashing into the soft sheets. "Wake me up in four hours."

A short time later when I wasn't sleeping but obsessively replaying the day's events and Mark's observation, I heard the boys talking.

"Have you discovered anything else?" Logan asked.

"No," Mark sighed. "I wish it could tell us more."

"We will get him back," Logan stressed.

"I know," his voice made me think there was much left unsaid. I kept my breathing level, not wanting to disturb their conversation.

"Is it true about Lorraine?"

Logan grunted, his weight shifting the bed beneath me. "Which part?"

"Did she really cheat on you with another shifter, and is Olie really protecting her and possibly your unborn child?"

"Unfortunately, yes to all of it."

Mark gave a low whistle. "What are you going to do?"

I heard Logan's head thump against the headboard. "Find out if the child is mine first, and honestly I haven't thought past that."

"But you are done with her?" Mark asked eagerly.

I could hear the rueful smile in Logan's voice. "Yes, I think I have kept her around too long. She wasn't always the power hungry, inconsiderate nuisance she is today. At one point I loved her. I thought—" His weight shifted. "I hoped she would return to the person I fell in love with. Besides, marrying a human would help with our PR."

"Maybe, but not that human."

Logan gave a long sigh. "I know." His tight response ended the conversation. Logan might be able to take criticism, but he was still an Alpha among alphas.

"Thank you, thank you for helping me get Jerry back," Mark whispered, his voice tense from repressed emotions I could feel from ten feet away. He cleared his throat before continuing, "You and Olivia have been spending a lot of time together."

Logan grunted a response.

"She is a worthy leader and mate," Mark offered tentatively.

"Alright matchmaker, that's enough," I declared. I scooted toward Logan on the queen bed, "Get over here, and shut up."

"Really?" Mark asked hopefully.

"Yes, I forgot how much shifters like to cuddle."

"What, Bear not offer you any cuddling time?" Logan jabbed. The insult hurt.

"No Logan, I wasn't after Bear for snuggles."

"Then what?" the asshole asked.

"To forget. Now are you going to tell Mark it's okay if he comes over here, or do I have to get up and go to his bed?"

Logan patted the warm spot my body had left and Mark eagerly curled his body around my own. It would have been romantic when he buried his face in my hair, except he was in love with Jerry and I was an emotional train wreck.

Logan lowered his hulking form down, leaning closer so the minimal gap I had left between our bodies vanished. His warm skin heating my own, I thought, here's hoping I don't have nightmares.

...

It was a subtle jerk that woke me up. Logan looked down at me, his brow furrowed.

"Did I snore?" I asked, feeling Mark's heavy arm around my waist.

"No, it's been four hours."

I grunted, pushing at him. "Move, so I can get up without disturbing him. He needs his sleep."

"You aren't waking him?"

"Not yet, but I have to pee," I hissed, slowly wiggling my body out from under Mark and shoving Logan at the same time.

He gave a low chuckle as he watched me hustle to the bathroom. I snatched clothing for the day before shutting the door behind me.

Dressed with teeth freshly brushed, I rummaged through my bag until I found my binoculars.

"Going old school on this one?"

I shrugged. "I'm curious as to what's happening. I'd like not to be caught unaware."

Logan nodded before taking care of his own morning routine. I sat in front of the window, watching the people coming and going from the coffee shop and art gallery. While I didn't think the latter had any connection to what was going on, it didn't hurt to look.

A pain of longing struck me as I sat there thinking about my last stakeout with Jerry at the strip club. While he may not have been up front about who and what he was, I liked him. He had my back and I wasn't going to let him down now. Everyone had a past, and it didn't serve any purpose judging him for it.

Logan pulled a burgundy armchair close to my perch on the dark gold and white striped couch.

"Anything?" he asked, lacing his fingers over his flat stomach.

"Not yet."

"Hungry?"

"Do you even have to ask?"

He laughed, picking up the phone and ordering room service.

I heard the shifting of a sheet as Mark got up, silently dressing and coming to stand behind me.

"Logan ordered breakfast, do you want to go check out the coffee shop?"

I felt his gaze on me. I lowered the binoculars, turning to meet his eyes.

"You trust me? I was certain there would be some speech about not being able to keep my shit together." His teeth ground on the last part.

Logan looked at me, waiting for my response, which was, "I trust you won't let Jerry down."

He nodded, jaw still clenched tightly as he looked out, arms crossed over his chest.

"Why don't I get breakfast down there?" he asked, eager to see inside.

I smiled. "Sure, I doubt Logan ordered enough for all of us, anyways."

Logan huffed, "Do you need the wax cleaned out of your ears? You heard my order."

I chose to ignore him. "You have your phone?" I asked Mark.

He nodded.

"Good, take pictures, but—actually, Logan why don't you accompany Mark and act like a couple taking pictures!"

Sometimes I'm a freaking genius.

The look Logan gave me said he didn't share that appraisal of my skills.

Mark covered his laugh with a cough. "I can handle it, Olie, but thanks for the offer."

He grinned suggestively and the surprise laughter caught me off guard. We were all saved from Logan's retort by the arrival of breakfast.

Mark slipped out, still sporting a small smile, as two carts were brought in.

"Please tell me you ordered French toast and donuts and pancakes and hash browns," my watering mouth demanded.

"Yes to all the above."

"Glorious food, come to mama."

I pulled a metal cart towards my perch, analyzing my sitting arrangement as Logan tipped the man, closing the black door after him.

"Can you move the couch?" I asked, already munching on a donut.

With an annoyed huff he pushed it around until it hit the back of my knees and I sat. "Good?" he grumbled.

"Hmm, maybe a little closer."

I got a solid whack that pushed me closer and my bite of donut down my windpipe.

Hacking, I glared at him though watery eyes. "Asshole."

"Prissy."

"Hey, I think you have me confused with your ex-fiancée," I retorted, propping my feet up on the windowsill, powdered sugar coating my hands. "I believe you prefer the term demon whore to describe me."

He exhaled loudly. "I'm sorry I've called you that."

"Why? It's how you feel," I replied, smearing chocolate donut frosting on my binoculars as I watched Mark cross the street to the coffee shop.

"Maybe once," he answered honestly, "but not anymore."

"Careful Logan," I warned softly, hiding behind the binoculars like the chicken I was. "People might start thinking we are friends."

Silence.

...

Logan and I devoured both carts of food in the five hours Mark was gone. Logan had texted him to make sure he was okay, but Mark just kept sending pictures of various parts of the shop, everything from the bathroom to the back alley.

I cleaned up my hands, face, and binoculars before snatching Logan's phone from him.

"What the hell, Olie?"

"Shh," I muttered, zooming in and out on the alley, squinting my eyes as I tried to bring up the memory of Jerry bound.

Chewing on my bottom lip, I confessed, "It's possible I saw Jerry on the top step and not in the storage room."

Logan moved to sit beside me on the couch. I tilted the picture for him to see while I manipulated it.

"I can see why. The concrete floor and backing are the same as the storage room."

"And The Oracle smartly only showed a snapshot of Jerry, very little background."

I chewed on my fingernail as Logan's phone pinged. He reached over me to grab it, getting to the message faster than I could.

"Did it look something like this?" he asked with a hard edge.

My mouth hung open as the picture The Oracle had shown me consumed Logan's phone screen. Jerry was looking away from the camera, blood on his white shirt and an angry slant to his jaw.

"Shit," I hissed, reading the message: We will trade your magician for your succubus.

"No," Logan bellowed, taking his phone away. I reached for it, slumping into the couch as he stood up, pacing. "You cannot give yourself over to those witches!"

I decided to sit this argument out, for now, letting him rage. Picking up my phone, I debated texting Mark. Deciding he had a say in this, I did.

I watched Mark trying not to run back to the hotel. He arrived far faster than he left, the double black doors cracking under his weight as he outpaced the electric lock.

He was panting, but I imagined it to be more from nerves than exhaustion. "We are trading me for Jerry, once Logan confirms date and time."

Logan growled low in his throat, "Losing you gives us nothing."

I raised a calm eyebrow at him. "The witches needed Jerry for contacting the Fae. If they want to trade him, then things are not going as planned."

"Why do they want you?" Logan asked, his caramel eyes hardened.

"Money, sex, drugs, more information on the Fae. Fuck if I know."

Mark watched our exchange silently, which was really in his best interest.

"And you think giving them what they want is a good thing?" Logan yelled at me.

"I think having Jerry being held hostage is worse than me being held hostage. I can't help him, Logan. But this way, I can get him out without bloodshed. We are doing this." My voice hardened, daring him to try and fight this out with me.

Mark whined.

"Stop, Olivia," Logan said, averting his gaze.

"Uh, what did I do?" I genuinely wondered, blinking my gaze away from him to check on Mark.

Mark cleared his throat. "You were acting like a mated pair and I could feel your dominance through Logan."

"Huh, that's new isn't it?"

"Yes," was the enlightening answer from Logan.

I wanted to take issue with what he wasn't telling me, but we were on the clock. I got back on point. "Answer the message, agree to the trade."

Logan held his phone so tightly I thought he was trying to break it. Finally, pissed off, he typed a quick response before throwing the phone at me.

"Happy?" he hissed.

"No, Logan. I'm not." I left out that broken succubi like me don't get to be happy. Our endings are like our beginnings: bloody and brutal.

Instead, I handed him his phone, not looking at it when it vibrated again. His stiff shoulders pulsated with repressed anger. I stood with a huff, placing my hands on the skin of his biceps, letting my emotions seep into him, my resignation and possibly a little apology for pushing him so hard.

"How do they even know we are here? That we tracked him?" Logan questioned, ignoring my touch.

"I don't know," I sighed. "It stinks of a mole, to be honest, and I'm not sure whose House they're in."

"I will be okay," I uttered, taking a guess at what was bothering him, letting my confidence and peace with this situation seep into him.

His shoulder relaxed slightly as he looked into my eyes. Message sent. "Tonight at midnight, in the alley behind the coffee shop."

I have no idea what possessed me when I gave him a small smile and caressed the side of his face, his stubble pricking my fingers.

Thankfully, Mark was there to clear this throat. "Guys, you are killing me here."

"Sorry Mark," I giggled, not exactly sure what I was apologizing for. "Let's order food. I'm starved. "

...

I had stuffed myself with every dessert item on the menu, plus a grilled cheese that Logan insisted I needed to eat. Whatever.

We sat together on the couch, me dressed in my leather pants, soft white shirt, and matching leather vest. It was a new addition from Myrtle and could hold almost double the usual number of throwing knives. Not that I had any weapons on me at the time. I was actually debating changing back into jeans, but that seemed like a nervous twitch and I didn't want to give Logan any ideas.

Mark sat on my left, he and Logan both in jeans, not needing more weapons than their claws and fangs. And they wondered why I was jealous. Their legs leaned against mine, protective and worried.

"We should go," Mark stated tentatively.

I patted his leg and stood.

The walk to the coffee shop was uninteresting, through the fancy lobby, past the glass doors held open by a polite doorman. We made our way steadily and I wished it could have taken longer. The "what if's" were playing on repeat in my head. What if Jerry was dead? What if the witches had already contacted the Fae? What if I was leading the Alpha into danger? What if, ... ENOUGH. I had made my decision and I would accept the consequences.

As we rounded the corner into the alley, my eyes were drawn to Jerry on his knees, about ten paces in front of several black hooded figures and Destiny, hood back. Smiling.

"So glad you could make it," she greeted us merrily.

"I'm going to enjoy killing you," I informed her. Her delicate laughter had me reaching for blades that weren't there.

"Now, now, succubus." She smiled, throwing her dark hair over her shoulder. "I knew the Alpha was too smart to keep your troublesome ways around."

Logan's lips peeled back in a snarl. "Let's get on with it."

"Fine, enough small talk. Send the demon whore to Jerry."

I walked without having to be told, keeping my gaze trained on Jerry, whose lip was dripping fresh blood. Reaching down, I helped him stand, balancing him when he swayed.

His head dipped to my shoulder. "Forgive me," he whispered.

"There is nothing to forgive," I whispered back. "Can you make it?"

He nodded and I moved to allow him past me. Mark struggled to stay next to Logan, pain etched deeply into his face, as Jerry stumbled toward them. I turned toward Destiny, not seeing the reunion.

But I did hear Logan command, "Get him to safety."

I steeled myself to walk to the witches, but Destiny's features darkened.

"What are you doing?" she shrieked at Logan.

I turned, seeing him next me. "Logan, go!" I hissed at him.

When I looked again, I saw that it wasn't the Logan I was used to interacting with. Seeing his lion peering back at me, I gulped and quickly averted my gaze.

The witches fell back, leaving Eli sauntering toward us, his flunkies not far behind.

"Logan?" I asked softly.

A growl was his only response.

Eli's eyes were wild, and if I didn't know better I'd say his beast was running the show. The click of a gun had me turning my head to Logan. The barrel of a large caliber weapon rested against his temple.

"It's fucking silver, bitch. Screw with me and I'll blow his head off. He won't be able to regenerate."

"What do you want?" I asked, unable to look away from the gun.

"Fix him," his voice broke with painful emotions. "Fix my father, Eli."

Slowly, I turned back as Eli circled in front of me. "I can't fix this."

"You can and you WILL!" His desperation turned into conviction.

Eli shifted into wolf. The transformation was breathtakingly fast; not even Logan could duplicate it.

"They spelled him," the gun wielder announced, "to make him shift faster. But it's destroying him."

Slowly, I lowered into a crouch.

Logan spoke one word: "Don't." His eyes flashed with heated anger.

I shook my head with a groan and kneeled in front of the shifter. His silver eyes held no human emotions, only an idle curiosity. He turned and huffed to the man holding the gun to Logan's temple.

This was going to hurt. Resignation hunched my shoulders as I reached out to fist my hand into his fur. A pull from a shifter in animal form, while courting the possibility of succumbing to the shifter's beast, hurt.

A pull from the results of magical enhancements, I'll admit to being a little scared at that thought.

Sucking in a long breath, I pulled the wildness into my soul. My back arched of its own will, the animal nature seeking a release. Fear, confusion, and hatred blasted through me, finding a voice in my throat. There was too much; behind my closed lids I could see the magic, watch what I pulled out filling back up just as quickly.

Fuck.

I kept pulling, squeezing my eyes closed against the pounding in my head, the pressure building from the foreign emotions.

Grinding my teeth, I squinted an eye open and saw my work have an effect as the silver eyes gained human intelligence again. Stemming the flow of raw emotions, I tried to wrench my hand free, finding that my fingers would not obey me. The wolf snapped far too close to my face, the magic roaring into him once again.

"Olivia, STOP!" Logan screamed.

Turning my neck took more effort than I had in me. Still squinting, I saw Logan was free. With a heavy woosh of air, I tried to release my hand again, finding it once more refusing the commands I gave it.

The silver wolf snapped at my shoulder.

I had to get away. I had to dump some of this rage or I would be worthless to get us out of this situation. Terrified necessity had connections firing inside of me that I didn't take the time to understand, only encourage.

When the flow reversed into Eli, I was shocked. A warning buzzed in my ears but I ignored it, expelling all of the unfiltered, powerful hatred I had absorbed.

Granted, I pushed emotions all the time, but they were my own and I played upon others' existing emotional states. This was different, and it was uncontrollable for me. The rush drowned out all other noises, blinded my eyes yet again, and forced another scream from my lips.

But it didn't stop. My own emotions rushed out, as pain, betrayal, and anger tumbled down my arm and into the silver wolf. It was too much, the power of the witches fueling him plus my own turbulent emotions. I felt his life force snap under the brutal assault.

Gasping for air, I released the wolf, pushing away from him, shock numbing me. I had killed him with a touch? Where the fuck had that talent been hiding?

A distant part of my brain was worried. This was succubus magic. This was my true magic.

Darkness blocked out the rest of my thoughts, exhaustion claiming me.

...

I rolled over, my head pounding, knees grinding against the harsh cement.

"Fucking hell," I hissed, pulling at my chained wrists. "Not again."

"My thoughts exactly," Logan answered.

"Seriously, they got us both?'

"Yes."

"Crap, now who is going to save us?"

Logan looked down at me with a raised eyebrow. "You typically free yourself."

I sighed. "I was going to play the damsel in distress this time, see if the sex was better."

Logan laughed, pulling at his own chains.

"Mine are magic," he informed me, holding the chains to the minimal light for me to see.

"Mine aren't." I gave a tug but nothing happened.

"Wanna try?" I asked, holding my chains to him.

He shook his head. "I have a shorter tether."

I groaned.

A deep chuckle reached my ears and Logan turned, not surprised to see a shifter with a striking resemblance to the silver haired one I had killed standing in the shadows.

A little warning would have been nice.

"And you know what?" I added defiantly, "When I get out of here I'm fucking killing the maker of these chains. I've seen this shit enough."

The shifter worked his way into the room, perching on a discarded wooden box.

"I had hoped it wouldn't come to this, Alpha. You have left me no choice but to follow through with my father's plans."

Logan growled, stretching the chains with a hopeful creak.

The lanky wolf smiled smugly. "Don't bother."

"You are unhinged just like Eli was," Logan warned. "Release us, and I won't kill you brutally."

He shrugged, peering into the darkness behind us. I turned, searching but not finding anything, before turning back warily.

"You have ruined the packs," he began in a trance. "You must be stopped. Under the full moon's glow the witches shall reach the Fae and set this right."

My blood ran cold. He was insane and well connected, fucking perfect.

"Oh, and the metal is spelled. I don't recommend pulling on it anymore." With that he took his leave.

Logan pulled on the chains again, brutally. The muscles in his arms threatened to snap the seams of his shirt.

"Don't shift," I warned him.

He grunted before trying to shift. The effect was immediate, his breath sucked in between clenched teeth, his face paling. "Olivia," he whispered, his normally enchanting eyes glowing sick bronze laced with fear.

"What's happening?" I asked, kneeling before him, placing a hand against his own.

Power flung me back, only the chains keeping me from flying farther. "Ouch," I groaned, holding my head. Bouncing against concrete was certain to leave a lasting mark.

Logan ripped at the chains, logic and mental clarity gone. Groaning, I pushed the pain down deep, crawling back to his side.

Being prepared for the blast this time didn't make it any better. Keeping my body as low to the ground as possible, I touched his hand again. Power blasted into me, shocking my senses and leaving me a writhing ball of pain, but still I held on. Once I had the pain braided down to allow brain functions, I felt what the witches had done.

Anger, rage, and lust blasted through the chains into Logan, pushing his lion half precariously close to turning beast.

"No," I commanded him, grasping his forearms and trying to stop him from pulling insanely against the chains. It was useless; Logan was a powerful shifter. The man could have stayed calm and contained, but the lion would never stop fighting.

Interesting to note the similarities to Nari's operations. Dammit, had I missed something? Or rather, someone?

My muddled brain made fast deductions that I wasn't willing to look at closely. I moved my hands to wrap around Logan's rough knuckles.

"Hold on," I whispered. Closing my eyes, I began pulling.

"Shhh," I tried calming him, unable to hear my own voice above the roaring in my ears.

The emotions were easy to lock away, to trap and seal into metal balls in my head. The problem, aside from my burning hands, was that the draw wasn't stopping. Pushing my awareness outside of myself, I focused on the cuffs.

While I had told Darren I wasn't magically inclined, even I knew I had somehow been able to pull magic in from Stephen, the Puppet Master who forced me to interact with the overgrown kitten on a permanent basis.

"I've got it, Logan, just stay with me." He probably scented the lie, but I was desperate to keep him sane.

Purple tendrils wrapped around his wrists, sliding up his arms, pulsing with raw power. Moving my hands, I touched the restraints. It burned, flaying my nerves. My hands were sizzling, the scent of burning flesh causing Logan to buck even more wildly.

Tears leaked down my cheeks as again I pulled, drawing the magic into me. An echo, vision or memory had me seeing the purple eyes of the witch in the cave where I rescued Blake, and since I didn't believe in coincidences, I'd be paying her a visit, you know, right after I regained feeling in my hands.

Blowing out a breath, I cracked a blurry eye at Logan. His raw sienna eyes were wide, staring down at me. My body swayed down, my muscles unable to keep me upright. I thumped again onto the hard concrete with a groan. At least it wasn't a long fall this time.

"What did you do, Olivia?" he asked, confused.

"What I do best." I gave an attempt at pushing up, but my hands had curled into themselves. "Suck."

Crap, I walked right into that one.

Logan cleared his throat, his calm detachment forced back into place.

"Are the cuffs still spelled?"

"Nope," I groaned, the concrete suddenly very comfortable.

...

I woke up with a lion standing over me. I refused to be embarrassed about the gasp and squeak that left my mouth.

Caramel eyes drifted down to me, humor twinkling in them as he licked my hands with a rough tongue. "Ow," I groaned, shifting onto all fours under him. The choice to lean against his furry arm wasn't from lack of strength.

The weight of the chains was gone, replaced by the throbbing in my hands. Repositioning myself so I could look at Logan without getting cramps in my neck I asked, "So, for your first time being captured with a succubus, is the experience everything you expected?"

He lowered his nose, huffing into my face.

"Alright, I'm getting up." Grabbing a fistful of fur, I clamped down on a whimper and hauled my body off the floor.

"Fucking witches," I hissed.

...

I went first on the stairs, mainly so that if lion-sized Logan broke them I wouldn't be stuck. Secondly, because I needed to do some damage. The rage I had absorbed demanded an outlet and I was only too happy to accommodate.

We had found a healing salve in a container of miscellaneous ointments, and while my hands weren't back to normal, I could unfurl and use them. Okay, so the witches may have a few, and I stress a few, uses.

I pushed the door open a crack with my shoulder, crouching down to peer on either side before moving it farther. The door swung easily and granted, if I hadn't had my head pounded against a hard surface twice in the last 24 hours, I might have questioned that.

But I didn't, which was exactly why I got grabbed by some wolf flunky.

"Logan, RUN!" I screamed. The four hundred pound lion bounded up the steps, only to have the steel door slammed and locked in his face. Fuckers were prepared, I had to give them that.

I bucked, thrashed and was just generally difficult in the flunky's grasp.

Eli's son yelled for more men to hold me.

It took three. If my hands weren't injured, it would have taken more. Eventually, I was forced to kneel, bleeding from a busted lip and broken nose, as Destiny moved toward me.

"Difficult," she advised me.

"Bitch." Not my best comeback, I'll admit.

"Remove her," the witch commanded the shifters.

"Taking orders from witches now."

The asshole with a chokehold on me pulled my hair back, exposing my neck, his nose drawing down to inhale deeply before he whispered in my ear, "You survive this, and you are mine."

"She won't," Destiny said, moving around the small, dusty kitchen, gathering her supplies.

"I will say I am impressed by your father's knowledge of the girl. I never dreamed a worthless succubus would have the ability to absorb so much power."

Eli's son nodded absently, his eyes watching me closely.

"Had we more time I would have loved to discover the origins of her power and what else she can do."

I turned to the side and bit down forcefully on the thick arm around my neck, drawing blood. He didn't let go, but he did make me go to sleep. My last thought was that Logan should really stop pounding into the door.

...

I was bound, again. On my back this time, with rope securing each of my appendages, held taut by thick stakes.

Fucking hell.

The night sky glittering above me was the only thing I could see as chanting reached my ears.

"She rises," a musical voice muttered before its owner moved into my vision. "You possess a position of great honor among our kind. You will be the bridge to reach our families." Pale hair peeked out from her black hooded robe, touching my face gently.

"You are a fool," I hissed.

"Karma, come away from the sacrifice," Destiny called out. I twisted, trying to see her, but my limited vision wouldn't allow it.

Karma looked confused by my words. Tilting her oval face at me, she reached down, pressed a finger to my forehead, and pushed. Magic exploded behind my eyes, white in color, pure in intensity. My natural guards grabbed it before braiding it and shoving it down deep.

When my vision cleared, Karma smiled. "You are the perfect sacrifice."

I groaned, closing my eyes. This was not good. These assholes knew more about my magic than I did and unless Logan got out of his cage, I wasn't going anywhere anytime soon.

Great, more time with the witchy bitches.

Their chanting lulled me; calm stole upon my limbs and I relaxed, watching the sky with resignation clawing at my heart. I always knew the life I had chosen as an Executioner wouldn't be a long one and if this was how it ended, I couldn't bring myself to care.

Eventually, Grams would send out a party to look for me or Darren would hunt down his brother. They might be too late to save me, but I had confidence they would stop the witches and free a pissed off Logan.

Destiny moved above me with an impressively wicked hunting knife.

"Begin," she whispered. From my side, the witches formed a line, repeating the same thing Karma had done, touching my forehead and shoving. Some shoved quite a bit, others nothing more than a spark. I closed my eyes, seeing the colors bloom and absorb into the pit filling up in front of me. The color darkened slowly into an oily darkness, coating my insides until it demanded a release.

I really wished the new skill of killing someone by pushing my emotions—okay, possibly magic—into them was something I could summon on demand.

My back arched of its own accord and I pulled on the ropes again. They moved ever so slightly, digging into my wrists and ankles. I wrapped my hands around them.

Destiny crouched in front of me, the blade above my heart. "If only someone had bothered to train you. You would be the greatest magician the world would ever know," she whispered.

Someone had taught this bitch how to cut, for she sliced vertical cuts up my arm, deep enough to burn but not life threatening. Using the same blade, she sliced off my leathers at the upper thigh, cutting close to my femoral artery, allowing my blood to flow freely. This was an impressive torture technique. I'd have to remember it, pending survival of the blood loss.

The chanting began anew, calling to the magic inside of me, summoning it to thread out above my head. I blinked as their voices formed the magic into a spinning circle. My warm blood spilled over my wounds, soaking into the ground.

"It's working," Destiny breathed, the knife lowering to her side, wonder in her eyes.

"ITS WORKING!" she screamed, the wind whipping around her. I wanted to struggle, but the heavy tide of magic had me feeling as if a giant was kneeling on my chest, pinning me to the spot.

The circle turned into a sphere, cracks of white piercing the darkness. The witches continued their chants, having to scream to be heard above the howling cyclone that was forming.

A face appeared for only a flash and my body stilled. If that was whom they called, I wanted to die and I wanted to die now.

The sphere moved next to my body and a booted foot stomped onto the ground. Seven feet tall, with a black cape and blood red breastplate, he looked every bit the gladiator coming to the rescue, but I knew better. He was a barbarian.

"Four," he oozed, his voice grating on my nerves. "It's been some time, pet."

I pulled against the bonds, feeling the rough rope slice into my wrists, warm blood flowing faster from my wounds. His steps moved away from me, and though I hadn't seen his face, I remembered it well. A decayed skull sat upon his shoulders, black orbs for eyes and sharp, sharp teeth.

My head thumped against the ground and I let the tears fall from my eyes, unashamed. The witches had unleashed into this world the monster I feared the most. We were all dead.

A soft touch had my eyes snapping open. "There, there, Four, all is not lost."

"Bob," I whispered to the short, twig-like man as he moved away from me.

"Now, Luharposn, take your pick. The Queen has only allowed us a short time here."

"Pity." The gravelly voice had me pulling against my bonds again, sending a fresh wave of pain through my body.

"No, we called for Bob." Destiny's voice sounded panicked.

She knew the name. She had seen my memories.

"Bob is a peacekeeper. You cannot call him, nor can you choose whom you call, you pathetic half-breed."

So she was right about being part Fae. I wished that mattered.

Bob tapped his foot impatiently, crunching the dead leaves under foot.

"I want Four and—" I squeezed my eyes closed, refusing to let the whimper of fear leave my mouth. The others would be safe: Grams, Tommy, Mindy, Harrison, Kass and Hannah, they would be okay. Bob would make Luharposn leave. Even if he took me, even if he delivered a fate worse than death, I would keep my loved ones safe. I blew out a breath, my struggles ceasing.

"If you take Four, you cannot have anyone else," Bob negotiated.

"I dislike your rules, Peace Keeper."

"I'm aware, Luharposn, but these are the Queen's rules. If you take Four, that is all you can take; if you take the others instead, you may have them all."

"Fine," Luharposn ground out.

In a blink the clearing was deserted, the inky blob disappearing into the night sky. I sagged against the bonds, relief flooding through me as the tears dried up.

A roar penetrated the brief silence, followed by an eerie howl.

"Please be help," I groaned, lifting my head to search the area I thought the noise had come from.

Logan's angry form sprang into the clearing, moving slowly when he saw only me pinned down.

"A little help!" I called out, trying to mask my shaky, strained voice.

Not sparing a look at me, he sliced the ropes holding my legs before moving to my head. Pulling my body parts in close to my core, I sat up too fast, blinking away black spots.

Leaning my head on my knees, I blew out a breath, savoring the fact that I could do so after how close I had come to a fate worse than death.

Logan shifted forms, kneeling down next to me. "Olie."

"He was here," I whispered, my body shaking against my iron will.

"Who was?" Logan asked, searching the area.

"He's gone," the words a brush against my lips; I was losing the battle against unconsciousness. "He took them all, new play things. I was an old play thing."

He crushed me to his naked chest and I've never been so happy for my cheek to be shoved into a sweaty shifter chest.

…

I awoke slowly, groggily, to Logan's hands running over my open wounds.

"They aren't deep," I slurred, trying to sit up. "It's more exhaustion."

I groaned, putting my head between my knees. "How far are we from the house?"

"Not far, can you walk?"

I nodded, pushing off the soft ground made damp by my blood.

"I'm going to shift, I'll be able to detect threats faster."

I nodded, pulling myself back to my own two feet while Logan made the transition. The large lion butted up against me, helping to support my weight.

I'm pretty sure Logan's take on distance was wrong, because we walked until my wounds soaked through all my clothing. When the tall porch steps finally came into view, I was close to passing out from both exhaustion and blood loss. Up the four steps I pulled myself, using the faded blue wooden handrail, collapsing on the final step.

Logan shifted again and walked by me, hopefully to check out the house. My eyes drooped closed and while I knew I shouldn't give in to the temptation to sleep, I'm fairly sure I did, awakening once Logan picked me up.

"Humogh."

"That's not English. I found keys, we are leaving."

Sounded good to me.

...

Soft bedding under me was a contrast to the multiple pricks of pain in my body.

"Oww," I moaned.

"Don't move!" shouted two voices.

Cracking an eye open, I looked down to Logan stitching up my leg and Mark tackling my arm.

"Where's Jerry?"

"Sleeping."

I grunted, "Is he okay?"

"He will be," Mark answered. "We need to stop your bleeding."

I nodded, resting my head down again.

"What a fucking night," I whispered.

"It's not over," Logan warned.

"More Fae?" I couldn't handle that.

"No, Angelina called while we were hostage. It appears the package is being moved."

"Fucking hell."

"I figure we had best go after her before that happens."

"There is no we."

"You need to learn how to accept help," a weak voice out of my line of sight stated.

"Jerry, you just work on getting better, asshole. I plan on beating the crap out of you. Those fucking insane witches contacted the Fae."

"I can actually only claim partial fault in that," Jerry strained, ending in a cough. "I had the knowledge, you had the power."

I sighed, wanting to deny it, but knowing better. "About that. Destiny, while slicing and dicing, said something to me." I paused, working up the nerve and giving myself a breather as Logan started on another slice. "She said if I was properly trained I'd be a magician."

Jerry cleared his throat. "Don't even think of getting up," Mark warned, his hands not stilling at his task.

"I'm not surprised, Olie," Jerry grunted. "The entire coven poured their magic into you in order to contact the Fae and you didn't die. That, to my knowledge, has never happened before."

I grunted.

"What happened to them?" Logan asked.

"He took them," I whispered, clearing my throat only to find my fear. "Luharposn."

I felt Mark's hands still on me. "Is he gone?" he asked, his terror evident.

"I think so. Bob said the Queen would only allow him to either take me or the witches, not both."

I felt Mark's squeeze on my hand.

Chapter 17

"I'm coming with you," Logan growled. I was able to score a few hours of sleep before I had to do Angelina's dirty work.

"The hell you are," I responded, quickly walking away from him. Mark and Jerry were renting a car for their trip back to St. Ann.

With little difficultly, which annoyed me, he stopped my progress, spinning me to face him. "It wasn't a request."

While I could play the bitch card here and tell him it wasn't any of his damn business, and what I did to tie up loose ends with an ex and his deranged mate was my problem, there was a bigger issue.

"You can't, Logan." I softened my eyes and my stance. Something about having a near death experience with the man had changed our relationship, or maybe it was what The Oracle had said, either way I wasn't dwelling on it.

"I am going to take out an entire vampire House, without permission, to save Blake's niece. You, as Alpha of the entire US, cannot be involved. The risk is too grave."

He moved his sexy self mere inches from my face, breathing out warm and fragrant breath. "You are part of that leadership as well, not to mention you have your own Supernatural Council to attend to."

Mesmerized by those tawny golden orbs, I confessed, "They'll be fine without me. They won't be without you."

He pulled back, a half smile on his lips as his fingers trailed down the side of my face, sending warmth to places it shouldn't. "I'll never understand why you don't value yourself."

I shrugged, his words tossing cold water onto me.

"You are still—"

He moved faster than I had given him credit for, pressing those blush colored lips against my own. Shock stole my breath and stilled my movements, before firm pressure had me returning the kiss with equal enthusiasm.

One swipe of a tongue against my lips had me opening, allowing him passage as we twined around each other. My hands stroked the well-defined muscles under his shirt without my permission and I really wanted to sling a leg around his hip to bring our pleasure parts closer together.

I could feel his smile under my lips and I pulled back, my breathing annoyingly irregular.

"What the fuck was that?" I asked breathlessly.

"You might not remember our first kiss, but you will remember that one."

I could only huff as an answer. I had seen The Oracle; stolen memories are kind of her thing.

"Not to mention I just won the fight." I swear he fucking preened.

"Asshole," I hissed, my eyes narrowed, despite the smile tugging at my lips.

"I'm driving," he announced, loading up our bags.

...

She was waiting for me, well us, the vampire bitch. Someone had tipped her off and I was going to take one guess as to who.

"Angelina."

The blonde smiling before me was Patricia Bellarosa, the color of her hair clashing with the amber of her eyes. Her perfectly white fangs bit delicately into her full bottom lip.

"Very good," she said, bouncing her foot crossed over her knee, examining her perfectly polished nails. She was giving me a break, considering two of my wounds had opened up and the split lip she had given me was also bleeding freely. I wasn't ashamed to say I was taking the reprieve. I leaned heavily against the wallpapered wall.

"Now, I bore of this." She stood, smoothing her skintight suit. "The sooner I kill you, the sooner I can get out of this horrid state."

The dwelling she was currently kicking my ass in was not the farmhouse I had envisioned. Nor would I call it horrid. Wait a minute.

"It wasn't your idea to come here? Angelina orchestrated the pet problem?" I tapped my head against the wall behind me.

The goon next to Logan relaxed slightly. He and Logan had come to unspoken agreement on not getting involved.

She scoffed, "Of course, she wanted Blake and she was going to have him. You were a mere stepping stone to securing him. Although I will say you dispatching Gregory in such an effective way surprised us all. Don't think she has forgotten about that. Once you are gone, the rest of your vile line will pay for it."

I laughed.

"You think this is funny?" she yelled at me, using her vamp speed to yank my head by the darkly dyed roots.

"I do," I admitted, blood dripping into my eyes as I stayed against the wall.

"You are beaten, bloody, and near death. Admit defeat."

I laughed again. She wasn't wrong, but she didn't know me very well.

"I tire of your games." Snarling, she revealed her pearly white fangs, angling her head to slam into my jugular.

Silently thanking Tommy and his movie obsession, I pushed the toe of my boot against the floor before kicking the blond in the chest with the dagger hidden there.

It wasn't a killing blow, but it bought me the time I needed. Her grip relaxed in my hair enough that I could push my body weight against her, causing her to stumble and lose her hold on me entirely.

Breathing heavily, I stood over the injured blonde. Her shock made me smile.

"I've never believed in giving up," I explained, before cleaving her head from her shoulders with my blade.

...

"This is a bad idea," Logan told me as I stormed up the steps of the manor to Tommy.

We'd had the conversation over and over on our way back here, but I didn't care. I needed answers.

"Pull it up," I asked softly in Tommy's room. I had called ahead to tell him what I wanted.

He was staring at me and I wasn't looking at him.

"Olivia," he whispered.

I turned to the sound of his voice. He never called me that, ever.

"Are you sure?" he asked again.

I nodded, the muscles of my throat having locked down from the threat of tears.

Tommy nodded, hitting play on the video on his computer. I recognized the venue instantly, the elegant and upscale restaurant from a night that had replayed over and over in my mind. The noise was gone and I could only see the diners from a far off distance.

Tommy pointed at a table in the corner before zooming in on the image.

The tears I had been holding at bay trickled down my face. Suddenly, my publicly humiliating breakup made perfect sense.

Angelina had wanted a front row seat.

I slammed every door on my way out.

...

Blake's niece was still passed out in the backseat of my SUV, though my shifter helper was gone. Sliding behind the wheel, I fought my instinct to crush the gas pedal to deliver her.

I was stopped at the new guard station, demanding to see Tate when the bastard pulled up behind me. The guard said something to him quietly and he got out of his hundred thousand dollar car, walking to my open window.

His sigh of annoyance said it all before he spoke. "Olivia, what do you—" he stopped, his eyes on the form in my backseat.

He gave orders in a language I didn't understand, and the burden was taken out of my vehicle.

Tate looked at me, wide-eyed. "My debt is paid," I said softly. He nodded and I turned and drove away from all of it.

I wanted to say more. I wanted to tell him he fucking drew the god damn line in the sand and I was going to kill them all. But he wasn't the cause of my pain. Angelina was, and I wasn't done with her. I believed what Patricia had said, that she would come after those close to me.

The good news was, I planned on taking her and her House out first.

Chapter 18

It was a peaceful evening on the porch of the manor, which undoubtedly meant someone was up to no good. I lacked the motivation to investigate further, pulling another long drink of my wine.

"You really are better off without him," Kass reassured me, patting Harrison's back as he slumbered against her.

I saluted her with the bottle.

Shaking her head, she laughed at my attempt to change the delicate subject of my broken heart. I wasn't doing too well with dealing with it, actually I wasn't dealing with it or even allowing myself to think about it.

I was absolutely drinking about it, however, when I was supposed to be watching the kids and Mindy while Grams enjoyed a date night with Mercer.

"You weren't yourself with him."

"Who was I?" I slurred out.

Kass leaned back in the wicker chair, staring up at the stars, taking her time to answer. My eyes drooped from excessive alcohol consumption.

"You were the girl you thought you should be," she finally answered, turning to look soberly at me.

I gulped, knowing I wasn't going to like this probe into my emotional state.

"You were happy and giddy and overlooked a lot for him because you thought you should, because you wanted to be loved."

I pulled a long drink, not looking at her before I answered, "You shouldn't know me so well."

Standing carefully with her precious cargo, she put a hand on my shoulder, gently squeezing. "You are not alone in wanting to be loved, Olivia."

I huffed a non-answer as she went back inside to check on the kids.

I might not be alone, but I don't deserve it. I do not get a happy ending. My job, my one sole purpose, was to protect those like me and my ending would be bloody and slow.

Mindy wandered out a few hours later, crawling into my lap.

"I hate myself," she confided in me.

Hello, prodigy.

"No, you don't. You hate not being strong enough to get out of a bad situation."

"I hate everything," she whispered tearfully. "No one could possibly understand. They try in that stupid victims class Grandpa makes me to go, but they can't possibly."

I turned to her, setting the cold beer down. I had to help her.

"It will get better."

"No, it won't. Don't lie to me."

I cringed. She was right. "Fine, here's the truth. The nightmares will wake you for the rest of your life, innocent moments will flare painful memories, and you are right, no one fucking understands." I sighed.

"Isn't there a 'but' coming?"

I looked over at her with a raised eyebrow.

"You feel that? People have called it different things over the years, fight, attitude, determination, but I've always called it hope. The simple truth is, though they abused your body, what they did in no way diminished your power. You are not less because of what happened to you, if anything you are more. You have gained a strength many will never have, a resiliency unknown before, and while you will always fight the demons that now have free range inside of you, you will do it with skills and power few can share.

The tears slipped down her cheeks, soaking into her cream shirt.

I slipped an arm over her shoulders, not drawing her close.

She leaned into me, securing her small arms around my waist.

"It gets better?" she asked, muffled.

"Yes," I answered, stroking her hair, "and someday you will find someone who can love all the pieces of you, even the broken ones."

She nodded, taking comfort in my words. Hopefully for her it would end better.

www.ingramcontent.com/pod-product-compliance
Lightning Source LLC
Chambersburg PA
CBHW022107170626
46808CB00002B/644